D0906778

HEARTS ARE WILD

*A River of Dreams
Romance*

Other books by Heather S. Webber:

The *River of Dreams* Series

Surrender My Love
Secrets of the Heart

HEARTS
ARE WILD

•

Heather S. Webber

ANDERSON COUNTY LIBRARY
ANDERSON, S. C.

AVALON BOOKS
NEW YORK

© Copyright 2004 by Heather S. Webber
Library of Congress Catalog Card Number: 2004090295
ISBN 0-8034-9667-2
All rights reserved.
All the characters in this book are fictitious,
and any resemblance to actual persons,
living or dead, is purely coincidental.
Published by Thomas Bouregy & Co., Inc.
160 Madison Avenue, New York, NY 10016

PRINTED IN THE UNITED STATES OF AMERICA
ON ACID-FREE PAPER
BY HADDON CRAFTSMEN, BLOOMSBURG, PENNSYLVANIA

To Gram,

Always encouraging, always accepting,
always giving, always loving.

This one's for you.

I miss you.

Chapter One

Cincinnati, Ohio 1894

Thick white plumes of cigar smoke clouded the west room of the Maybury, Cincinnati's famous gentlemen's-only gaming hall. It was nearly impossible for Jack Parker to see her own hand, never mind the face of her rival across the poker table.

Which was just the way she liked it. If she couldn't see him all that well, then he couldn't see her either.

All the same, she tugged the wide brim of her cowboy hat down lower, to cover the fine features that would surely give her identity away. There was no disguising her full lips, her creamy skin—curse it—despite how hard she'd tried over the years to hide the traits she shared with her two sisters.

Slumping into an artless slouch, she stared at the cards in her hand. Three aces, a two, and a five. Her gaze skipped to the pile of chips on the table.

The raucous roar of games being won and lost echoed behind her, but Jack barely paid attention. Her focus was solely on her cards and the heap of money on the table.

1

Usually, she didn't play for stakes so high, content to add to her kitty a little at a time. Tonight, however, she had been careless, a little wild, and more than a bit reckless.

It was entirely Cal McQue's fault.

Perspiration dampened her brow. She didn't dare wipe it away. She could upset her Stetson and locks of her long dark hair might escape. That wouldn't do. She'd perfected the art of looking like a young man from her clothing to her walk, but she never could bring herself to cut her hair in a short boyish style.

It irritated her that she held that one bit of vanity, but after being nurtured all her life by a father who raised his girls as if they were sons, her hair . . . well, her hair was one piece of her femininity with which she didn't want to part.

It lay heavy on her head, coiled beneath her hat and pinned mercilessly tight. Still, the locks seemed to have a will of their own and Jack often found herself tucking back stray strands when no one was looking.

The man across the table breathed heavily, his girth trembling with each deep exhalation. Pale lamplight danced across his bald head. So far, she'd won seven out of their ten hands. He was having a hard enough time losing to a *boy*. He'd have an apoplectic fit and probably die right in his chair if he knew he'd been losing to a woman all this time. If he didn't die immediately, then at the very least, he'd have her kicked out of the men-only Maybury, minus her winnings.

No, that wouldn't do at all.

Those winnings put her one step closer to her own ranch. She'd found the land out near River Glen, where she had grown up, for a song. Although River Glen wasn't the vast Montana prairie she'd dreamed of since childhood, it would do. For although she was a loner at heart, she couldn't bear heading west alone. The land in River Glen would suffice.

It had taken an hour of begging and cajoling to get the owner, Mr. Searcy, to hold off considering other offers until the end of the month. She had two weeks to earn fifteen hundred additional dollars. And the pot on the table was just the beginning.

She slid the 'two' card across the table, face down. The dealer handed her another card. Slowly, she lifted it.

A three.

Drat!

She'd been playing poker for nigh on ten years now. Long ago she'd learned to hide her disappointment behind a bland expression. It was a trait that served her well—not only in cloudy gaming halls, but also in life.

The man across from her accepted two cards from the dealer, and unlike her composed expression, his jumping eyebrows gave away the fact that he had a good hand.

There was only one way for her to win that pot. She had to make him believe she had a better hand than he did.

Without hesitation, she tossed a twenty-dollar chip into the pile. "I raise you," she said in a gravelly voice that had passed as male many, many times.

The man, overweight by a good fifty pounds, spoke around his cigar. "Boy, I believe you're bluffing."

Jack shrugged noncommittally. Over the years, she'd found that silence was the best answer to any question. With dismay, she watched as he tossed a twenty-dollar chip onto the table, then added a fifty.

A flutter of panic passed through her stomach. If

she lost now, she'd lose a whole month of winnings. It would almost be like starting with nothing.

Hardening herself against unaccustomed anxiety, she tossed in a fifty chip. Taking a deep breath, she tossed in another fifty.

Sink or swim, her father had often told her. She just hoped she didn't drown. Ordinarily, she'd have folded by now. But she wanted that land. Enough to make her turn a bit wild, throwing good sense to the wind.

Seeing her sisters so happily married and content in their new lives had pushed her to satisfy her own personal ambitions. Oh, she was happy enough running the gaming room on the *Amazing Grace*, the steamboat she and her sisters had inherited from their father—the steamer they'd just recently turned into a floating hotel—but it wasn't what she'd had her heart set on since she was old enough to walk.

A ranch, all her own. Where no one could tell her what was right and proper. Where she could muck about in the stables and ride barebacked until she was spent.

It wasn't going to be easy to tell her older sister Alex, who with her husband Matt operated the boat, of her plans, but Jack was beyond changing her mind. She wanted her horse farm, and she would prove just how much a woman could achieve when she had her mind set on it.

She held little worry about the fate of the *Amazing Grace's* gaming room. Despite her feelings for the man at the present moment, the gaming hall would thrive and prosper in Cal McQue's very capable hands. Gambling was in his blood. How often had he told her his dreams of owning a club of his own one day? Too many to count. Not that she was passing her duties on to him to fulfill one of his dreams, she told herself. She was doing it for the sake of the boat, and herself.

The man across from her leaned in. All other players at the table had long since quit when the stakes had been raised, and slowly blended into the crowd, leaving her, Wheezing Man, and the disinterested dealer all alone in the back corner.

She slouched lower.

"What are—" He coughed. "—you hiding, boy?"

Hiding? She nearly bit out a laugh. One of the many reasons she was here tonight was to do just that. Hide. From the prying eyes of her concerned sisters and from those of her new brothers-in law. From Cal McQue, whom she hadn't seen in nearly three months. Cal, who had returned to Cincinnati from his family home near Louisville with another woman, Charlotte, he'd said in his letter, was her name.

Curse him.

She should have known he'd have a woman back home. Men like him were irresistible. As she well knew. Cal had always been full of mystery. Long before she'd met him formally, she'd seen him in this very club using a phony name—not that she knew it at the time. His charm and the hint of danger he carried had captivated her instantly.

Jack fought against the wave of self-pity that had been dragging her down this past month, ever since she received Cal's telegram telling of his return.

Today.

All day, she'd been avoiding the *Amazing Grace*, where Cal would undoubtedly live with his new sweetheart and resume his long-standing job as her brother-in-law Matt Kinkade's right hand.

All the more reason she needed to get out on her own. She couldn't bear to see Cal's quicksilver eyes all dewy over another woman. It was enough to make her sick.

She'd escaped the boat early that morning, well before anyone else was awake to note her absence and had yet to return twelve hours later.

For a while, she'd visited with her younger sister, Lou, and her new husband, newly arrived home from a wedding trip to New York City.

She'd stayed longer than she should have, listening to tales of the city, of all to see and do. She'd learned all there was to learn of John Hewitt's family, including an update on his ebullient grandmother, Mrs. Scranton-Regent. Jack had listened patiently as Lou told of how Daphne, the young woman who had become a friend to them all over the past month, was faring wonderfully after being taken in by John's grandmother. Lou had been aglow with love and good health, and though Jack was more than thrilled for her sister, she couldn't help but feel a stab of envy. There was so much she wanted. So much she could never have.

Lou, ever the meddler, had tried to pry information from her, disguising it with talk of the *Amazing Grace*, and of Alex, their older sister, who was expecting her first baby in a few months' time. Then the questions of Cal's return had slowly edged into their conversation, and Jack had fled to the safe haven of the Maybury, where all she had to think about was the ranch she longed to buy and not how she'd made a fool of herself over a man.

What are you hiding, boy? Peering under the brim of her hat at the man across the table, she simply shrugged off his question. "Do you call?" she asked.

The end of his cigar glowed bright red as he puffed.

Cheeks flushed, his hands shiny, he tossed another twenty-dollar chip into the pile.

She sighed inwardly. Stubborn men. They galled her like nothing else. Seeing his bet, she upped the ante. Another twenty. Only a few chips remained in front of her. This couldn't go on much longer.

From an adjacent room, a loud holler split the air, followed by a rowdy cheer. The Maybury's band began to play, a song full of sound, full of sadness.

Yet maybe that was just her take on it. Broken hearts did that to a person. She berated her foolishness for ever believing that Cal McQue cared about her in the first place. What did they share? Witty banter and a love of gambling. He'd never voiced any promises, but she'd heard them, in his eyes, in the way he looked at her.

Foolish.

Foolish to ever believe she could have what her sisters had found. She was much too independent, too set in her own ways. The sooner she could buy that land and forget about what she and Cal could have had the better.

Her bitten-to-the-quick nails scraped against the red velvet lined table as she pushed what was left of her chips into the pile. "I call."

It was now or never.

Wheezy's eyes narrowed on her, intense and angry. Would he call? Would he fold?

Her boot tapped a nervous rhythm and the fringe on her suede pants danced with apprehension. Then, after a long minute, the man threw his cards into the pile, sighing disgustedly.

She hated that tears suddenly sprang to her eyes. All her life she worked so hard to keep those annoying female traits at bay, and here she was about to bawl like a big old baby. Over a game.

Not just any game, though. Maybe the old farmer would take this money as a down payment on that land?

She raked the chips toward her and began stuffing them in the pockets of her duster, the one she wore whenever she came to the Maybury, whether it was ten degrees outside or one hundred. There were some things about her that weren't so easily concealed.

"Why're you wearing that coat, boy? You cheatin'?"

Cheating? There was nothing worse than being called a cheater. They were the lowest of the low, the rock bottom worst kind of coward.

Jack rose from her chair, stood ramrod straight, giving her tall frame even more height. Lowering her voice, she said, "You accusing?"

He must have seen something in her stance, heard a warning in her voice. "Nah."

"I didn't think so."

She turned to cash out her chips. Another holler rang out from the adjacent room. Curiosity got the better of her.

Four men were leaning over a poker table, all with sleeves rolled to their elbows, whiskey close at hand, and a mountain of chips separating them.

Sidling in for a closer look, Jack gaped at the winnings on the table. There had to be several thousand dollars in the pot.

Edging her way through the crowd of onlookers, she made sure not to bump anyone. Her curves were too generous to be mistaken for anything but what they were. And being caught now would ruin her whole plan. The Maybury had become her benefactor in a roundabout way, and if she were banned she'd never win the money she needed to buy her land from a thrown-together poker game in a squalid barroom.

"I fold." A small man with a perfectly trimmed beard pushed away from the table, stretching his arms above his head. "This is over my head."

"We'll miss you," a sarcastic voice said from the opposite side of the table. "Or at least your money."

Jack froze at the sound of that voice as the crowd roared. Smoke swirled and danced, blurring her vision. She poked her way through the crowd, snaking closer to the table.

Peering over a man's shoulder, she leaned in.

Cal.

A shot of warmth cascaded over her, heating her from the inside out. Seeing him again, so solid and masculine, turned her world on its ear. She'd tried to convince herself that she could just walk away from him, ignore him and he'd disappear from her life, her heart. But seeing him now, she realized it wasn't going to be so easy.

Her heart hammered in her chest as she took in his short, dark, wavy hair, the whiskers curving around his strong jaw, his tense broad shoulders. His blue shirt was dotted with marks of perspiration.

Jack watched as he lifted a hand to his hair, brushed unruly locks back with a quick swipe of deft fingers. For a moment his hand lingered, rubbing at his scalp as if he were in pain.

A burst of worry washed through her before she thrust it aside. He was no concern of hers. Not at all. He belonged to another. Charlotte.

His telegram echoed in her head.

Will arrive in Cinti via railroad on 15 June. Look-

*ing forward to introducing you to Charlotte. Don't
know what I'd do without her.*

Well, Jack darn well knew what she'd do without
this . . . this Charlotte. She'd fight for Cal. Because
other than her own piece of land, there was nothing
she wanted more. But not at the expense of another
woman. Even Jack had her boundaries and this was
not one she was willing to cross.

As Cal gazed at the deck of cards, his silver-green
eyes looked hard as stone, and his face held no color
at all, except for a slash of red where his lips pressed
together.

Unlike her game, there was no dealer here. The men
dealt the cards themselves. And apparently it was
Cal's deal. She watched as the man to the right of Cal
asked for two additional cards.

Blinking, she gaped. Surely, she'd been seeing
things . . . but no, she hadn't. Cal *had* dealt from the
bottom of the deck. Since she ran the *Amazing Grace's*
gaming room, and had been gambling since she could
add sums, she knew what to look for, knew what had
just happened.

Bottom dealing: cheating.

Shock cemented her to the floor. Blood rushed her
ears, making her feel light-headed.

Another player folded. And Cal's sole remaining
rival asked for a card. Again, Cal dealt it from the
bottom of the deck, with such finesse and ability that
it stole her breath. It took an accomplished con man
to be able to fool so many.

As if he could feel her eyes on him, Cal looked up,
found her in the crowd of men as if he'd known all
along where she stood, recognition widening his eyes.

Without so much as a blink of guilt, he stared at
her for a long moment. Behind her, a glass crashed to

the ground, shattering. People turned, but Jack kept her gaze riveted on Cal, on the table. Which is why she spotted Cal's opponent slip a card from beneath the table, add it to his hand, and then call.

She opened her mouth to protest, but snapped it closed. One cheater deserved another.

Cal laid his hand on the table. A flush. His opponent smiled as he bared a royal flush.

Men all around her clapped and cheered. Cal's gaze shot to her, his eyes looking old, the life she remembered in them gone.

She turned to go, refusing to feel sorry for him. All this time she'd thought she'd been the fool, when it had been him fooling her. Making her believe they shared something special. Making her believe he was a man of honor.

But he was nothing but a cheat.

Chapter Two

Pushing her way through the crowd, Jack cashed out her chips and headed to the door. She needed the night air to clear her head, cleanse her lungs.

Looking both ways she rushed across the street, dodging an oncoming surrey headed from the direction of the opera house. Her strides were long, quick, as she strode toward the Landing, where the *Amazing Grace* was docked. Normally she'd hire a horse from the livery but tonight she wanted the long walk, the fresh air.

She needed the time to think, to digest what she'd witnessed. She brushed hot moisture from her eyes, cursing it as she did so. Crying twice in one night. It was appalling.

Through the years she'd found herself a good judge of man. A quick glance was usually all it took to see if someone's character rang true.

Never, ever, in her life had she felt so deceived. She'd met Cal nearly six months ago, a night she'd never forget. A night she'd found him battered and bruised in her cast iron bathtub, soaking away his worries after Matt's steamboat exploded and he and Cal had had to jump into the river to save themselves.

She'd fallen for Cal's looks on the spot. And after she spoke with him, recognizing him from various gaming clubs around the city—to which he denied ever attending—her interest had peaked and she'd fallen for much more than his rugged handsomeness. She'd fallen for him. Hard and fast.

And now, knowing he was a cheat, her heart felt as though it had been ripped from her chest and stomped on beneath boot-spurred heels.

Somewhere in the distance, a trolley bell rang. Jack stepped up her pace. She might be dressed like a man, but she was still a woman, and what had happened to her sisters in the past few months had raised her alertness of those around her.

"Jack! Wait up."

She walked faster as Cal ran toward her. Her pace kicked up when she heard his footfalls coming closer, but she stopped dead in her tracks when a large form slunk out of the shadows, blocking her way.

"What's your hurry, boy? Off to spend my money?"

Wheezy! He must have been waiting for her all this time. In a rush, she went over the lessons of defense her father had taught her and her sisters. Through the course of her gambling years, she'd unfortunately had to make use of them a time or two. Unfortunate for the men who'd tried to steal her winnings, that is.

"Give me back my money, and I won't have to hurt you."

She was tempted to hand over the winnings that she'd worked so hard to earn just so she could slip past this man *and* be away from Cal.

Then thoughts of her land, of green rolling hills and wide open pastures sprung to her head. It offered her something she'd never had before. Freedom. Pure freedom to do what she wanted, how she wanted, with no one to tell her otherwise.

And if that picture had, before this night, included small children playing tag on the hillsides, children with their father's silver-green eyes and unruly hair and their mother's love of nature, who was to know it but her? And she'd never tell, never share the painful hopes and dreams she'd fostered for months.

Footsteps pounded behind her. Wheezy took a painful hold on her arm. "Just scoot . . . on . . . past us now."

Heavy breathing, shallow and ragged, pulsed against her neck, making her shudder.

"And mind . . . your own . . . business," the man said when Cal came into sight.

The street lamp cast a gloomy pall over the street and the curbstone. The summer sun had set hours ago, and a cooling breeze fluttered litter and leaves from stone to stone along the street.

"I don't think so," Cal answered, his eyes still lacking any warmth.

A ribbon of concern unfurled in Jack's stomach. What had happened to him? His eyes used to dance with mischief and mystery. Now they simply looked dead. What had caused the change?

It didn't matter, she told herself. She pushed her unease aside. He didn't deserve her concern.

"Just go," she said to him. She could take care of Wheezy on her own, if he didn't keel over first from lack of air.

"No."

A meaty hand tightened on her arm. "Why not?" *Wheeze, wheeze.* "He cheat you too?" He shook her, and she could feel tendrils of her hair slip down over her ears, sweep against her neck.

Cal's eyes turned granite hard. "If you hurt her, I will kill you."

"Her?" As if he'd been touching fire, the man yanked his hand back to stare at her, his chest rising and falling in dramatic fashion.

She glared at Cal. How could he? He had no right to go blabbing about who she was. If Wheezy squealed to the managers of the Maybury, how was she to earn the rest of the money she needed?

"You're a . . . a girl?" the fat man stammered.

Jack tipped her head so the light fell across it. Her chin lifted. "What of it?"

The wonder seeped out of the man's vision. "I . . . lost to a girl?" He stepped toward her, his chest heaving. Menace bounded into his eyes, his expression. "A *girl?*"

The sound of a gun being cocked echoed. The man froze as he reached for her. Cal said, "I warned you." He leveled the gun.

The man's hands shot into the air.

Something inside Jack sparked to life. A security she hadn't known for a long while. She was used to taking care of herself, handling her own problems. It was almost . . . nice to have someone caring for her.

"I don't see you running," Cal seethed. "And if you make mention of this, I will hunt you down."

Jack pushed aside all goodwill she might have allowed to briefly surface as Wheezy took off, hobbling down the street, calling out threats over his shoulder.

Turning to Cal, she watched as he slipped his gun into his boot and pulled his denim pants over it for cover.

She turned her back on him and stomped away.

He dogged her heels. "What? No thank you?"

Spinning, she came chest to chest with him, and a flutter of something new and unknown tightened within. She refused, however, to back up, to give an inch.

His chin lowered to accommodate her hat as she tipped her head up to look him straight in the eye. "Thank you?" she whispered. "Do you really expect me to thank you?"

For a brief flash, she saw the Cal she had once known, the kind, gentle Cal. Not the cheater.

She jabbed him in the chest with a finger. "You ruined everything!"

Cal grabbed her arm. With effort, he reined in his temper. "I ruined everything? That's rich." He laughed. The sound rang hollow. "It's *you* who ruined everything."

She angled her head to the side, and his gaze slid over the smooth creamy skin of her neck. Her big blue eyes were filled with anger, hurt and accusations. "You have some nerve." With a jerk, she freed her arm. For a long moment, she stared at him.

He thought she was going to yell, to scream at him like any normal woman would do, but Jack was far from normal, which was one of the reasons he'd taken a liking to her in the first place. Inwardly flinching at what he saw in her eyes, he knew he deserved no less than her derision. She'd seen him cheating. A part of him wanted to explain his actions, but he knew he couldn't. Even if she could forgive him—which he doubted—he could never forgive himself for stooping to the level at which he now crawled.

There was no turning back for him. Getting caught cheating wouldn't stop him from doing it again. And he would do it again.

He had to do it again.

Abruptly, she turned from him and stomped away, her boots clicking soundly on the curbstone running the length of the street. Her head shook as she went, and he could hear her muttering under her breath as he watched the sway of her step.

Long strands of her dark hair trailed out behind her, blending in with the dark night. The tails of her duster made a steady thumping noise as they met the heel of her boot.

Though he wanted to just let her go, he couldn't. There was no way he was leaving her out here alone. Not after what had just happened.

The sneer of the man who attacked Jack lingered. *He cheat you too?*

Cal clenched his fists. He was tempted to go back and find that man and finish him off. Calling Jack a cheat. There wasn't a more honest, sometimes brutally so, woman around. At least when it came to cards. And it wasn't that Jack lacked honesty at other times . . . It's just that she had a way of manipulating the truth to fit her needs, bending it until one had to look very closely to see the truth at all.

"Stop following me," Jack called out over her shoulder, picking up her pace.

"No."

This wasn't how he expected his homecoming to be. He'd thought she'd be waiting for him with a big smile and open arms. But when he and Charlotte stepped off the train at the depot, Jack had been strangely absent from those waiting to welcome him back, and Jack's sister, Alex Kinkade, bless her innocent heart, hadn't been able to look him in the eye.

Jack was up to something. And her absence told him

that it wasn't anything good. He should have known. She was nothing if not unpredictable.

It was just as well. He'd had doubts that he could have looked Jack in her warm eyes and broken her heart. Tell her that a relationship between the two of them would never work. He'd had a lot of time to think while he was at home, cleaning up old messes and making new ones of his own, and it just didn't seem right to drag Jack into any of it.

His focus needed to be on Charlotte right now.

A slight ache remained where Jack had jabbed him in the chest. *You ruined everything.* He sure as heck knew that she had ruined his game. After seeing her standing there, his insides had gone all to mush and his concentration had fled, allowing doubts to surface. Seeing her again made him realize letting her go wouldn't be so easy.

Biting back the shame at being caught cheating by her, he reached Jack's side in a few long strides. "What exactly did I ruin?"

The sky was dark and cloudy, not a star or sliver of moonlight to be seen, and the street lamps cast the barest of light to guide their way. Still, he could sense anger radiating off her in pulsing waves.

"Everything."

With a quick look, she crossed the street, never slowing her pace.

"I know you saw me bottom-dealing," he said to her back.

"It just supplements my already low opinion of you."

Her caustic words threw him for a loop. Already low opinion? She was mad at him *before* she saw him cheating?

His lungs were starting to burn and she didn't appear to be even breathing hard. "Why weren't you there to greet my train today?"

"Not interested."

Her words stung. Her rejection stung, but wasn't this what he wanted? To end their relationship once and for all?

Maybe it was, but he'd been the one who wanted to do the ending. It was for the best. Once, he thought he could gloss over his past and move on with life, but that telegram from Charlotte shook his world and made him realize that he couldn't easily leave his past behind. It trailed him everywhere he went, following him into barrooms, gaming halls, and even on the *Amazing Grace*, where he thought he'd be able to sweep aside who he had been, who his father had been.

His legacy foretold his choices in life. He had no say about it one way or the other. But he did have the power to save Charlotte's future, even if it meant backing away from his own, and the happiness he could have had with Jack.

Eerily quiet, the streets were all but empty this time of night. Lights shone from behind closed shades on locked storefronts. Cincinnati was all but a ghost town as a thick fog rolled in from the river.

Jack slipped down a wide alley that led to the river. Rats scurried in the shadows and still Jack didn't break her stride.

They reached the Landing, and Cal looked downriver to where the *Amazing Grace* was wharfed until its next journey.

He'd only had the briefest of moments to see all the changes on the boat, and he'd been astonished at the transformation. In a little over three months the *Amazing Grace* had taken on a new aura, a new purpose.

Matt had been holding a job for him, one he knew he had to decline, but had yet to find the courage to tell Matt so. One trip back home to Louisville and his world had given way beneath his feet.

The *Amazing Grace's* stacks towered upwards, merging into one in the dark, foggy night. Lights blazed from within the boat, and the stage was lowered to the Landing.

Cal reached for Jack's arm. They needed to have this out once and for all. Before they went onboard. After all, he was fairly certain Charlotte would be waiting for him, ready to give him what-for for abandoning her this afternoon.

At his touch on her arm, Jack jerked to a halt. "Let me go."

"I can't. Not until I know."

She sighed, tiredly. "Know what?"

"*What* did I ruin?"

Tipping her head to the side, she said dryly, "My opinion of you?"

He flinched, but he refused to apologize. He'd done what he had to do. He held tightly onto her arm. He didn't want her running off.

Darkness enveloped them like a blanket as the fog thickened. "And much more." Her voice cracked. "How could you?" she asked.

"I had to."

"Why?"

Water lapped at the cobblestone. "It's complicated."

She stiffened, put her hands on her hips. "How complicated is it to say to me, 'Oh, by the way, Jack, I have a woman back home, so don't get attached?' "

"A woman?"

"Don't act daft," she said, turning sharply and breaking free of his grip. "It doesn't become you."

He swore under his breath and reached for her again, getting a handful of duster for his effort.

Jack stopped, but didn't turn around.

Through tightly clenched teeth, he said, "I thought we were talking about me cheating."

Her foot began tapping a furious rhythm on the cobblestone. "Oh, well, yes," she drawled, "there's that too. Did I know you at all?"

He ignored her, still stuck on what she had said. "What woman are you talking about?" All women had been banished from his mind the moment he'd met Jack. She'd been lurking in his thoughts, his dreams for months now, taking up, he was beginning to dread, permanent residence.

Where in this great big, vile world did she get the idea he had a woman back home?

A soft feminine voice carried down the shoreline. Charlotte. He sighed heavily. He just didn't have the patience to deal with her now.

"Cal? Is that you?" Charlotte repeated, this time with more than an edge of anger lacing her tone.

Jack freed herself and clamped her arms over her chest. Even in the darkness he could feel her glare. Her toe tapped. "That woman, perhaps?"

Chapter Three

Out of the misting fog, the strike of heel hitting cobblestone came closer. Jack's throat clogged with fury. The gall of Cal to deny he had a woman when she was currently making her way toward them at a wobbling clip.

The fog parted, revealing a young woman, around Jack's own age—or maybe Lou's—and Jack drew in a deep breath. If this was Charlotte, she was lovely. Rings of golden hair caressed her face. Creamy skin glowed in the darkness, radiating good health. A ridiculously elaborate hat masked her eyes, but Jack could sense the woman's anger as she stepped closer, losing her balance, teetering on boots with heels too high.

Jack tamped down on her empathy as the creature came into full view. Those curls of hers were a knotted mess; her traveling dress was wrinkled beyond hope with buttons missing and tears at the hem from being stepped on; she held tattered gloves in one hand.

Jack felt rather smug for about a half second, before the woman launched an all-out attack on Cal. Then she just stood back and enjoyed.

"Cal, where have you been?" she cried out, her voice ringing sharply in Jack's ears. "You promised me you wouldn't run off and leave me. I excuse myself for five minutes—five minutes!—and you're gone. Poof." She poked him in the arm as if not truly believing he was standing there, his expression getting darker by the minute. "Disappeared. I won't have it, Cal. I'll get right back on that train and go home. With or without you."

If possible, Cal's scowl deepened. "You'll do no such thing."

Ferocity emanated from the woman's features. Her ruby red lips pursed into a thin line. Long lashes narrowed over blazing eyes. She reached out and pinched Cal. "Just watch me," she bellowed.

"Dammit, Charlotte!"

Oh ho! So this *was* the famed Charlotte. And although Jack was reveling in Charlotte's tirade against Cal, one of her words rang in her head, caught at her heart.

Home.

She had said she'd get on the train and go *home*.

What did that mean? Were they married? She saw no rings, but that didn't mean all that much.

Charlotte turned on her heel, wobbled, regained her balance and took a tentative step away from them and toward the *Amazing Grace*. Cal reached out and grabbed her arm.

Jack stepped in. "Let her go. She's obviously very upset with you, an emotion I daresay I know all too well. Perhaps she wants to be left alone."

Charlotte's chin shot up. "Yes, perhaps." She nodded in apparent righteous indignation.

"You women and your foolhardy notions." He shook his head. "I'll never understand you. Either of you. I don't have time for this," he mumbled, dropping Charlotte's arm. "Have you learned nothing with all your lessons?" he asked her.

"Pardon me, but my lessons are my own business."

"Not when I'm paying for them," he roared.

Jack's head spun. What were they talking about?

Her ridiculous hat wobbling, Charlotte huffed and puffed, and even that downright stupid feminine trait didn't offset her beauty. "I didn't want the lessons in the first place."

Cal's voice lowered to a deadly whisper, echoing across the foggy Landing, reverberating off the walls of the nearby warehouses. "Well, if this isn't a prime example of why you needed lessons to begin with, I don't know what is."

He turned to Jack. "I apologize," he said with great difficulty.

Charlotte's mouth dropped. "Are you apologizing for *me*?!"

"I am."

"You're a . . . you're a beast!"

Anger hummed from his throat. "So I've been told."

"Look," Jack said, not knowing how to be the peacemaker—that had always been Lou's job. "Why don't we go aboard the boat and settle this there?"

"What is wrong with you, Cal?" Charlotte demanded, bitter humor in her voice. "Where are *your* manners? Aren't you going to introduce me to your friend?"

Jack turned to him, watched him squirm. "Yes, Cal. Please do," she said, oh-so sweetly.

He held up his hands in surrender, though his coiled, bunched muscles revealed how tense he truly was. "Charlotte, *honey*, this is Jack Parker. Jack, this is Charlotte McQue."

Jack's jaw dropped. *McQue. Honey. Home.* Good heavens, he was married. The cad!

She reeled back to slap him. He grabbed her arm, held it tight, before she made contact.

"Don't."

The one word was enough to stop her cold. She'd heard rumors about Cal McQue, about his quick temper and quicker trigger finger, but she'd never believed them true.

If it weren't for something soft and yielding in his eyes, she'd be having second thoughts about those rumors. Still, this hard, rigid side to him proved that she hadn't known his true character at all.

The tic of his jaw echoed as he released her hand. She backed up. "You egotistical, lily-livered, good for nothing . . ." She searched the deepest corners of her mind for a word that would truly fit how despicable he was.

"Beast?" Charlotte supplied.

Jack nodded. "Beast! You're married," she said incredulously. "All this time and you're married!"

Charlotte's face drained of color. She turned shocked eyes to Cal. "You're married? *Married?!* You couldn't at least mention that to me? You forbid—*forbid*—me to get married until I'm twenty-five, but you can just traipse off and get married without telling a soul?"

Jack's heart clenched as Cal rocked back on his heels, smiled smugly. Oooh, how he infuriated her.

"I am not—I repeat, *not*—and never will be, married," he said.

Jack stumbled backward, confused. She pointed to Charlotte. "Then who's she?"

Charlotte's hand flew to her chest, her face awash in horror. "You think—" she gestured between she and Cal, "—we, us . . . We're married? God save us all. It would be a cold day in Hades before I'd agree to marry a man like *him*!"

"I'm wounded," he drawled. "Truly."

Jack shook her head to clear the confusion. "If you're not his wife . . . who are you?"

"Me?" Charlotte asked, throwing murderous glances at Cal's self-satisfied expression. "I'm his long suffering, and I do mean suffering, sister."

Jack nearly fell flat on her hind side. His sister? Sister?! Would her humiliation ever end this night? Would she have any illusions left unshattered?

"His sister?" she muttered, fighting the urge to escape.

"Yes." The beautiful blonde held out her hand, smiled sweetly. "Pleased to meet you. Jack, right? I've heard so much about you."

Jack took the small hand and shook it. Charlotte's skin was smooth and soft, so unlike Jack's own palms that were rough and abraded.

She was proud of her hands, of how hard she'd worked, but something in her tensed, giving way to an onslaught of sudden insecurity.

This whole night had been a wreck, save for the winnings in her pockets. All these weeks she thought Cal had tossed her aside like someone's old rag doll. She'd been angry with him for nothing, and if she had met him at the train, her anger would have been allayed, and her foolish notions of love and marriage might be alive and thriving.

Even now he loomed above her, tall and dark and oh-so inviting. It was easy to remember why she had fallen for him, and even easier to remember why she couldn't have him.

Because once a cheat always a cheat. There was no two ways around that fact.

"Nice to meet you," Jack said, and turned on her heel, brushing past Cal and all his overwhelming masculinity without another word.

Jack paced the small expanse of her stateroom, past the footboard of her rumpled bed, past Lou's vacant bed. She'd always craved solitude, peace and quiet, and was quite surprised to find herself missing her younger sister. Her chatter, her humming. Her infernally annoying way of nosing into Jack's life and feelings.

Truthfully, she could use someone to talk to. Someone who could look at everything and tell her what to think.

Cal, cheating.

She never would have believed it of him if she hadn't seen it with her own eyes.

Cranking open the small window beside her bed, she allowed the night sounds and humid early summer air to billow in.

She couldn't reconcile it. Everything she knew about him portrayed him to be honest, forthright. It shook her that she hadn't known him at all. Not that he was a cheater, not that he had a sister. What else lurked in the shadows of his past?

A wife?

But no, he'd said he'd never marry. And didn't that hurt just a bit too much too?

She rested her forehead against the window casing, looked out at the city blanketed in a dense coat of fog. Only pinpricks of lamplight glowed eerily through the thickness.

A soft knock interrupted her thoughts. Jack sighed. An inquisition from Alex the last thing she needed.

Frankly, it amazed her that Alex had waited so long to seek her out, to probe for answers to questions she couldn't even begin to fathom. Pregnancy must be doing wonders for her sister's self-constraint.

She threw open the bedroom door. "Look Alex—" she began, then broke off when she saw Cal, not her older sister, standing in the hall.

The boat rocked gently as she hardened herself against a wave of longing. Curse it! Getting over him was going to be the hardest thing she'd ever done.

And that was saying a lot.

He smirked, an upward tilt of his lips. "Not going to invite me in?"

"What do you want?" Her heart hammered a staccato beat.

"I want to speak with you."

"Why?"

She watched as he once again rubbed his scalp with long fingers.

A flash of sympathy flickered, then quickly died.

Jack held open the door, closed it as he walked past. He smelled of smoke and sunshine, an odd combination to be sure, but something inside her recognized it immediately and tightened in remembrance, in need.

Angry at her base reaction, she closed the door more forcefully than she'd intended. Two dark eyebrows slashed upward as he motioned to the door. "Aren't you afraid of your reputation?"

Surprise made her smile. "Do you remember me? Hello," she said, waving. "I'm Jack, the woman who spent nearly an hour alone with you in a steamy bathroom while you bathed. My reputation has been beyond ruined since I was five years old. Nothing is going to change that."

Jack and her sisters had been raised by Hiram Parker to think freely, act independently, and to seek all things in life that would make them happy. Things such as baseball, archery, golf, Astronomy, mathematics, and for her, horses. Things that all three siblings had enjoyed, but others saw as just plain strange for girls.

The people of River Glen, the small town in which she'd been raised, had finally started accepting her family, thanks in large part to Lou's husband, Reverend John Hewitt. It was an acceptance long past due, but Jack was afraid her forgiveness of their behavior would be long in coming.

"Still," Cal said, "you should care about what others think of you."

"Why?" Jack shook her head, leaned against the wall. "All that matters is what I think of myself. And I know quite well that nothing untoward is going to happen in this room."

Though he didn't move from his perch on the bed, Jack sensed a change in him: a slight relaxation, a darkening of those quicksilver-green eyes.

"Is that so?" he said softly.

Her mouth went dry. When he looked at her like that . . . She gave an inward shake to those feelings, those thoughts.

"What do you want, Cal?"

In a blink, he was back to his rigid self. It was a shame to see that passionate, dynamic man go. But it was for the best. For both of them.

I am not—I repeat, not—and never will be, married.

Yes. It was best if she just let it all go.

"I just wanted to explain. About Charlotte."

Jack folded her arms across her chest. "Why didn't you tell me you had a sister?"

She'd known from previous conversations that both his parents had died, his mother when he was quite young and his father just a few years back, but that was all he'd ever mentioned of his family. Why would he keep Charlotte secret?

He rose from the bed, crossed the room and picked up a small bronze horse-shaped paperweight. Finally, he said, "I don't like speaking of my family."

Oh. What could she say to that?

"Charlotte's angry with me for bringing her up here, but I didn't know what else to do with her. I certainly couldn't leave her at home. She's too vulnerable."

Vulnerable? To what? "You speak of her as though she's a pet."

He shot her a dark glance. "She's barely twenty and already has been in more scrapes than I have in all my thirty years. Do you know why I had to rush back to Louisville?"

Jack shook her head.

"Because she ran away from Mrs. Garrison's Finishing School. Again. This is her fourth time."

Jack clucked. "One would think that you'd have gotten the hint that she's not happy there."

With a thud, he replaced the paperweight on her desk. "Her happiness is not my concern. Seeing her well prepared for society is. She's been very . . . spoiled."

"She seems like a perfectly charming girl. Bright, too." Charlotte had certainly recognized Cal's dark nature.

"She wants to wear pants, stay out late, mingle with hoodlums."

An icy finger of dread skittered up her spine. Hurt

like she'd never known ballooned in her stomach, pressing against her lungs, making it almost impossible to breathe.

Aching, she cleared her throat. "So you want her to abandon who she feels she is, her true character, to become a *lady*. A prim, proper, perfect coiffed, *boring* lady."

"Exactly."

Her hurt billowed, squeezing her throat. "Someone," she said, her words scratchy, "someone the precise opposite of me."

His eyes widened. "What? No, Jack, you misunderstand."

Jack flung open the door. "I understand perfectly. I think you should go now."

Traitorous tears stung her eyes, and she wasn't sure how much longer she could hold them in. There was no two ways around it. She was becoming a blubbering idiot. There was little worse.

"Jack—"

She turned from him. "Just go."

With a heavy sigh, he stepped into the hallway. Jack closed the door quickly, leaning against it for support.

The night—the whole day for that matter—couldn't get much worse.

She swiped at a wayward teardrop as a knock sounded.

Spinning, Jack yanked open the door, ready to do Cal bodily harm if he was standing there with more of his *explanations.*

Surprise jolted her as Charlotte stood on tiptoes, peering into the room. "Is he gone?"

"He?"

"Cal."

"Er, yes."

"Good." She brushed past Jack carrying a large leather suitcase and an oval hatbox. She set them both on Lou's bed, and proceeded to divest the suitcase of its contents.

"What are you doing?" Jack asked.

Charlotte looked up at her with wide green eyes. "Why, unpacking, of course."

Of course. How silly of her. She'd thought this was *her* room. "Why? Weren't your own quarters acceptable?"

"Oh, lovely. Truly." She tucked a ruby colored blouse into Lou's empty armoire.

Jack's patience thinned. "Then why are you here? In *my* room?"

Bright green eyes gazed at her beseechingly, fluttered. "Oh, you don't mind, do you? It's just that I hate sleeping alone. I'm used to the chatter of a roomful of girls."

"I do not chatter," Jack felt compelled to point out.

Charlotte pulled that hideous hat she'd worn earlier out of the hatbox, walked over to the open window and tossed it out. She wiped her hands. "A fitting death, don't you think?"

Jack couldn't help but smile. "Undoubtedly."

Charlotte blinked prettily. "But don't tell Cal. He paid a small fortune for that revolting thing."

"My lips are sealed."

She smiled. "Good. I'm forever indebted."

How could Cal want to change his sister? She was a perfectly lovely girl with a great sense of humor and a zest for life that rivaled few others. To stuff her into a world where she wouldn't fit would be a travesty. It was her duty to make darn sure that didn't happen . . . and she knew just where to start.

She closed the door. "You know, Charlotte is a perfectly nice name, but it doesn't suit you at all."

With sure fingers, Charlotte sought the pins in her hair. "I've never thought so, either, but there's nothing to be done for it."

"A nickname."

Charlotte's eyes lit. "Really?"

"Absolutely. How does Charley sound?"

She clapped. "A boy's name, just like yours and your sisters'?"

"Just like us," Jack said emphatically. "Strong, suitable."

"I love it!" She pulled her lip into her mouth, then released it. "But Cal's going to hate it." A smile blossomed. "Which makes me love it even more!"

Jack laughed. "Charley, we're going to get along quite well."

With Charley's help, Jack was going to show Cal just how *wrong* he could be.

Chapter Four

Cal had awakened early, a leaden sensation taking root in his stomach. For years he'd worked on steamboats, from the tiniest of cargo packets, to grand, elaborate steamers. And for years, he'd worked for Matt Kinkade, a man who had become more than just a boss to him.

He wandered the halls of the *Amazing Grace*, stalling for time. It was because of Matt and their strong friendship that Cal stayed on the river as long as he had.

Not one to sit still very long, as a young boy Cal had always envied the rivermen he'd seen while visiting downtown Louisville. The river beckoned to him, with its constant moving water and ability to take him from one place to another. And to be paid for his wandering? Well, that was just added compensation.

As soon as he was old enough to leave the ranch, he'd hired on the Sallie B., a cargo packet that traveled the Ohio and the Missouri Rivers.

The river life wasn't for everyone. Long nights and often lonely days, but he'd savored it . . . for a while.

And though Cal been born with gambling in his blood, the many towns along the river had fostered his passion; he wanted nothing more than to open his own place. But beyond needing to care for Charlotte, his name had prevented him from acting on his plans. The name *McQue* wasn't a welcome one in gambling circles, which is why he'd adopted assumed names since he was old enough to understand why he needed one.

He supposed his discontent with river life started when the *Muddy Waters*, Matt's previous steamer, exploded. It took the sense being knocked into Cal to realize he wasn't happy. Not with his job. Not with his life.

Yet, he couldn't figure out how to change it, until he'd received that telegram from Charlotte, then that visit to the Double C from Daley Lombard.

Now he had no choice but to change.

Gritting his teeth, he strode up one corridor, down another. He took in all the changes made to the boat while going over in his mind what he was going to say to Matt. How he was going to let him down.

Every lame, trite excuse Cal conjured rang hollow. The truth, however, sounded entirely too pathetic to even mention. He had to refuse Matt's generous offer of a job because Charlotte needed a nursemaid: someone to look after her, keep her out of trouble. And to keep her from accepting the attentions of all the wrong men.

Helping Charlotte run the family ranch, the Double C, shouldn't feel like punishment. Yet it did. He loathed ranch life. The long, tedious hours. The monotony—how it invaded your life, sucked you in, and never let you go.

Just thinking of it caused him to sigh raggedly. He was going to hate every minute he spent herding cattle.

But he'd do it, for Charlotte. To keep her safe. And away from that slimy, no-good Daley Lombard.

He ground his teeth together and the dull pain in his head blossomed into an all out throb. For weeks now, ever since Daley had come to see him with that infernal debtors note, the pain had kept him company.

He'd hoped coming back to Cincinnati would alleviate it, but so far it hadn't. In fact, it had only gotten worse. Thanks to Jack.

Climbing a set of wooden stairs leading to the Hurricane Deck, he thought about Jack, making the throbbing in his head double its pace. He'd really made a mess of things where she was concerned.

The hurt in her eyes the night before almost undid every vow he'd made to keep his distance from her. The truth of the matter was that Jack Parker was more of a lady than any prim, proper, *boring* society belle he'd ever met. But she'd also had a tough life, rife with rumors and whispers behind her back. He didn't want that for Charlotte. And he'd do everything in his power to see it didn't happen.

If that meant turning his little sister into a prim, proper society belle, then so be it. Eventually, she'd find herself a suitable young man who would take the time to get to know her and all her idiosyncrasies, love her in spite of them, and they'd live, as those dreadful fairy tales always predicted, happily ever after.

As sure as he was breathing, Cal knew two things. One was that Charlotte's prince charming was not going to be one Daley Lombard, and two, that if Daley Lombard ever forced Charlotte's hand, Cal would kill the man. Without hesitation.

The metal rungs of the steps leading into the pilot-house groaned in protest under his weight. Through the glass, he could see Matt sitting at the lazy bench, a newspaper spread before him.

Taking a deep breath, Cal rapped once on the open door and let himself in. All the windows had been cranked open, allowing a cross breeze to flow through the small, glass paneled room. A dormant stove stood in the center and Cal skirted it as Matt looked up.

Matt folded the paper, looked up at him with that infernal sparkle in his eyes. Gone was the haunted look that had plagued him since Cal first signed on with him.

A flutter of jealousy tramped over his heart, causing just enough pain for him to wince. It had been Alex, and her love for Matt, that had produced the change.

Would he ever find that kind of peace? He'd thought so right up until Daley Lombard altered the course of Cal's life faster than a swift current could send a steamer into a sandbar.

Flexing his fingers, he leaned against the enormous pilot wheel. Matt drew his ankle up onto his opposing knee, leaned back. "Wake on the wrong side of bed?"

"Is there a right side?" Cal muttered.

"I see. Don't suppose you want to talk about it?"

Talk? No. He didn't even want to think about it. He shook his head.

Matt grunted.

Cal's head pulsed a steady painful cadence as he thought about the note Daley Lombard had presented him with. He snorted inwardly, remembering that they once had been friends. Until their fathers had become adversaries.

"How's Charlotte? Is she settling in?"

"Settle is such a strong word, don't you think?"

Matt's eyebrows arched. He gestured to a small table in the corner of the room. "Coffee?"

"Alex didn't make it, did she?"

Matt laughed. "No. She likes you. She wouldn't want to see you poisoned."

Cal's stomach twisted sharply. How often would he see Alex or Matt once he returned to the Double C? Their life was here, on the river, and he doubted he'd have much opportunity to travel once he set his mind to running the daily operations of the ranch.

"I'll get it," he said, already heading for the server. He hoped to Saint Pete that it was strong enough to deaden his headache.

He poured two cups, the whole time acutely aware that Matt was watching him, trying to figure out what was going on. It wasn't right to leave him in the dark. Despite how much he dreaded turning down the job offer, he had to do it. Another man would have to be hired to replace him and there wasn't much time to find someone.

The coffee scorched his throat as it went down. Thanks be to heaven it was strong. "I have some news."

"Oh?"

Using the toe of his boot, he scuffed at the plank floor. The mug warmed his hands, though the rest of him remained chilled, despite it being hotter than a greenhouse in the small room.

"When the *Amazing Grace* leaves here to journey to Louisville, Charlotte and I will be on it, but we won't be taking the return trip back."

Matt sat quietly, waiting. It would have been much easier if he'd ask questions, jump to the correct conclusions, but that wasn't Matt.

"I need to offer you my resignation."

Matt stood. "I see."

"No, you don't." He stared out the window, his gaze

taking in the Kentucky waterfront on the other side of the river. "I need to go home. To stay."

"Does this have to do with the telegram from Charlotte?"

"Partly."

"Is there trouble? Anything I can help with?"

Cooler now, the coffee held no power over the ache behind his eyes. Using the heel of his hand, he tried to push away the pain. "Nothing you can help with."

"But there is trouble."

"I can handle it."

Matt set his mug down. "But you don't have to do it alone."

Cal turned to face him, saw the concern in his eyes. It humbled him, this friendship, but he couldn't burden it. "I know. But there's not much you can do. I've got to go back and take over the care of the Double C."

"What happened to Grogan?"

Grogan had been running the Double C since before Cal had been born. "Getting old against his will. It's time someone took care of him for a change. Not that he'll ever retire from ranching. He loves it too much to let it go."

Matt nodded. "What else?"

Leave it to Matt to know that there was more going on. "Nothing," he lied. Coffee sloshed over the rim as he set his half-filled mug on the table.

After a moment, Matt said softly, "What about Jack?"

What about Jack? Such a simple question, yet he didn't know what to say. There was nothing simple about Jack or what he felt for her. He bit his bottom lip, shrugged a bit. "We had a falling out. She won't even miss me."

Matt looked at him as though he doubted the truth

of the statement, but didn't comment on it. "We'll hate to see you go."

"It's time. Steamboat life was never a permanent one for me. I've stayed longer than I probably should have. Not that I didn't like the work, the business end, the figures and such. But the aimlessness of it all . . ."

"It's not for everyone."

"It's been an adventure."

The corner of Matt's mouth tipped up in a half smile. "It has."

Cal held out his hand and Matt hesitated for a moment before taking it in silent acceptance. A rush of surprise emotion hit Cal, making him tuck his hands in his pockets and hurry his departure.

Outside, the heat of the day bounced off him, like the sun's rays off the river. He swallowed hard, hating Daley Lombard for all the trouble he'd created, and for making Cal see that he was no better than the one man he despised more than anything, his father.

Jack didn't like to think herself a coward. She took risks more often than not, spoke her mind freely, without reservation.

Then why was she having a devil of a time figuring out a way to tell Alex she was leaving? She stood outside Alex and Matt's quarters, her hand poised to knock, her heart thumping in her throat.

With a deep breath, she knocked, the sound echoing down the empty hallway.

A mumbled 'come in' came through the thick wood.

Jack pushed open the door and peeked into the room. Still in her bedclothes, Alex sat on the rumpled bed, a notebook in front of her and a pencil perched between her teeth.

It was so unlike Alex to still be in bed this time of

morning that Jack immediately worried. "Are you well?" she asked, closing the door behind her.

"I'm fine. Just tired."

"Then you should be resting."

"You sound like Matt."

"He's right."

"I'm in bed, aren't I?"

"Doing work, it looks like."

Alex sighed, then brightened, her brown eyes sparkling. "Sit down, Jack. Tell me all about Cal's return. You must have seen him by now."

Jack took in the disarray of the bed, the duo of pillows with matching indents and fought back an intense wave of envy. She sat on the bench at the foot of the bed. "I've seen him."

"Then you know Charlotte is his sister, not—"

Jack held up her hand. "It doesn't matter who Charlotte is. Whatever I believed Cal and I shared . . . Well, I was wrong."

Alex straightened, the pencil gripped between whitened fingers. "No. We all saw it."

Shaking her head, she said, "We were all wrong. Can we just leave it at that?"

Alex had never been one to let things drop, but Jack hoped just this time she would. Unfortunately, she didn't.

"He cares for you."

"I don't want to talk about it." She couldn't bear to repeat the things he said last night. All the many reasons he'd listed for not loving her. Not that he'd come out and said so, but how else was she supposed to take his comments?

She hadn't thought him so narrow-minded. Had believed him to be one of those rare men who could look beyond image. She'd been wrong. So wrong about everything, including the caliber of his character. He'd proved that to her quite well.

"Okay. We won't talk about it. Not right now, at least."

"Thank you."

"Have you met Charlotte?"

Jack picked at a piece of thread hanging off the cushioned bench. "Actually, she's sharing my room."

Alex's eyes widened. "How'd that come about? There are plenty of empty quarters."

Jack shrugged. "Chatter."

"Chatter?"

Nodding, Jack said, without explaining the strange comment, "But it's fine. I don't mind the company and Charley is a wonderful girl."

After the initial shock of it all, Jack had been glad for Charley's company. *Yet . . .* Jack worried her lip. Long after Charley thought Jack was asleep, Jack had heard her crying. What was making her so unhappy? Cal? It was a good guess, but just that. A guess. She wanted to ask, but didn't feel as though they knew each other well enough to pry.

Alex scooted closer. "Charley?"

"Her new nickname."

A smile bloomed on Alex's face. "And how is Cal dealing with that?"

"He doesn't know."

"Ah." She tapped her pencil on the palm of her hand. "It does seem as though he's a bit unyielding where she's concerned. Don't you think so? Did you get that impression when you met with him?"

"I really don't want to talk about Cal."

Alex sighed. "I tried."

"I know you too well, Alex, to be caught off-guard by your rapid questions."

The thread she tugged on snapped. She sought another to pull off.

"Before you unravel my furnishings maybe you can help me?"

Jack straightened. "What's wrong?" She'd known something was wrong, with Alex still being in bed and all.

"I'm worried."

"It's not the baby, is it?" Jack's hand instinctively sought her empty womb. Her fingers curled into a fist with the ever-present realization that she would never have children springing into the forefront of her thoughts. She'd never know those flutters of life within her body.

She pushed the painful thoughts aside, as she always did. Some women were meant to marry and mother. She was not. It was high time she accepted that fact.

"Oh, the baby's fine." She patted her slightly rounded stomach and smiled.

It seemed as though the walls of the boat were slowly closing in, had been for weeks. She needed to get away, to wide open spaces where she could just breathe.

"Then why are you worried?"

It was rare to see Alex agitated to any degree. It was Jack who took on the worrying, shouldered it silently, let it burrow until her stomach hurt. Usually she tried to deflect the worry, help with whatever was going on, and she suddenly realized that she was about to add to Alex's worries with news of her leaving.

She couldn't do it. Not yet. She had weeks still until she moved into the small ranch house on the land she planned to buy. Until then, she would stay and help Alex with whatever burdened her sister.

Alex sighed. "The *Amazing Grace*."

"What about it? I thought these journeys were doing well, making profit."

"They are. A bit goes toward paying the crew's wages, some toward keeping up the high quality services we provide, and some toward the maintenance on the boat. But what remains after that is hardly worthy to bring to the bank."

Jack knew this to be true. The final profit was split between the three sisters. Although Matt had bought the boat outright from them a few months back, he had seen to it that the *Amazing Grace's* ownership was returned to the three of them after he and Alex had decided to make their marriage of convenience real.

"But still," Jack said, "it is money in the bank."

"It is," Alex agreed. Her eyebrows furrowed into a 'V'.

"You're still worried."

She looked up, her dark zigzagging curls tumbling forward. "What happens during the winter? When the river freezes and we have nowhere to go? We all thought we'd save enough during the warm months to get by, but," she gestured to the notebook in front of her, "the numbers aren't adding up."

Feeling her stomach churn, Jack swallowed hard. The lack of profit really wouldn't affect Jack all that much, not with her setting out on her own, or Lou, either, now that she was married, but the boat was all Matt and Alex had. Beyond being their home, it was their livelihood, and now that their family was expanding, they needed to think of the future. "We'll think of something."

Alex tapped the pencil against her lip. "Actually, I have thought of something, but I don't know how well it will be received."

Oh, she didn't like the sounds of that. "What is it?"

Leaning behind her, Alex reached for something. A moment later, she placed a section of newspaper in front of Jack. "I saw this in yesterday morning's news and thought it might just work."

Jack scanned the page, not sure what she was looking for. It was the society portion of the paper and there were grainy photos of the well-to-do attending various functions. She recognized a few of the faces as men she'd won money from playing poker.

"What do you think? Will it work?"

"Alex, I have no idea what you're thinking. I see nothing here that has even a vague link to steamboating."

"This." She tapped the lower left hand section of the paper.

Jack read the article, her eyes widening. "Oh no. You're not thinking . . ."

Alex beamed. "I am. It would work. We'd be docked here anyway, and we already have a ballroom."

A ball? Jack shook her head. She just couldn't see it.

"It would be a novelty, something special to do once a month during those winter doldrums. We'll charge a fee for entrance and provide lavish entertainment."

Dropping her head into her hands, Jack sighed. Wearily rubbing her eyes, she knew that Alex had already made up her mind. And Lou? Lou would agree to this nonsense in a heartbeat, which meant that her vote was unnecessary.

"I think, though," Alex continued on, "that we should have a practice run." She stood. "Yes, the last Saturday of the month—a week before we're due to leave for Louisville. That will give us plenty of time to spread the word and prepare."

"That's less than two weeks away."

"Plenty of time."

Knowing Alex, it was plenty of time, but still . . . "Does Matt know about this?"

Alex looked at her sharply. "He'll agree."

"It's crazy."

"It'll work."

"It'll work, but it's crazy."

"Maybe so." Alex smiled. "But I like crazy."

Jack had to laugh. Only Alex. "All right," she agreed, surrendering without a fight.

With a quick hug, Alex said, "We need to design invitations and talk about decorations."

Jack inched toward the door.

"Oh, and a theme. We need a theme. A costume ball? Fire and Ice as they do in Chicago? A Midsummer's Winter Ball?"

Jack closed her hand on the doorknob. She needed to escape before Alex ensnared her in her web of preparations. With a gentle tug, she inched the door open, crept backward out the door while Alex continued to ramble on.

She pulled the door closed as she backed into the hallway, relieved.

Spinning, her relief vanished as she bumped straight into Cal's unyielding chest.

Chapter Five

Backing up, Jack wondered if she could sneak back into Alex's room as easily as she had snuck out.

"D—did you need Alex?" she asked, pressing her back against the wooden door behind her.

The little space between them wasn't nearly enough. It seemed as though all the air had evaporated, leaving her short of breath and surrounded by Cal's scent. Pure sunshine and musky male—this time of day devoid of the usual smoke. That same base instinct sprang to life, making her want to reach out and touch him, run a finger over his knotted brow, trace the faint lines bracketing his down-turned mouth. Resolutely, she clasped her hands behind her back.

"Cal? Did you need Alex?" she repeated, noting the somewhat lost look in his eyes.

"No. Yes. I don't know."

Several strands of soft tufting hair spiked up as he laced his fingers behind his head.

Swallowing hard, she watched the pulse beating in his neck. Slowly, she raised her gaze and was taken aback by the wild panic in his eyes.

47

"It's Charlotte. I can't find her. I've looked everywhere. Her bed hasn't been slept in." He paused for breath and continued on, his voice scratchy and strained. "Have you seen her?"

Jack pushed forward, away from the door, a shot of fear scorching across her chest. "Not since this morning," she said, already walking toward her room, Cal's panic quickening her step.

Once she would have thought them all safe onboard, but that miserable fallacy had been proven wrong in the past few months.

"You saw her this morning? Where?" He dogged her heel. She could practically feel his warm breath on her neck, raising the tiny sensitive hairs there.

"She was sound asleep when I went out. I can't imagine she's gone far, if anywhere at all." She needed to tell herself that, will herself to believe it.

Grabbing her arm, he stopped her mid-stride. "When you left?" He shook his head. "I don't understand."

Oh.

She'd forgotten he didn't know that Charley had changed rooms. Inwardly, she winced. Cal wasn't going to be happy. She cleared her throat. "Charley's sleeping in Lou's bed." Pasting on a bright fake smile, she added, "She's my new roommate."

Color swept up his neck, over his bobbing Adam's apple, past that thumping pulse point and rushed into his cheeks. *"Charley?"* His eyes blazed with fierceness.

She drew her shoulders back, lifted her chin. "Yes, Charley."

He took a step back, opened his mouth, closed it again. His tone rising, he said, "I—I don't even know where to begin."

Holding up her hands, she said, "If you're about to stammer your way into a blistering tirade, I suggest you save it for someone who will actually listen to it."

She walked on, some of her anxiety easing away, replaced now with anger. Not at Cal this time, but at herself. How could she still feel something for him? It was almost as appalling as her recent tendency to cry like a newborn child.

Stopping in front of her door, she slid the key into the lock, heard the tumbler fall as she turned.

She knocked in warning as she pushed open the door. "Charley?"

The room was empty, both beds made. Jack checked under Lou's bed, saw the suitcase beneath it.

A wash of relief swept over her. Charley hadn't run away at least, but that didn't rule out other, more sinister, reasons for her absence.

Jack's gaze swept over the room, looking for any sign of where Charley may have gone, and it landed on a piece of paper weighted beneath the bronze horse on her writing desk.

Walking to the desk, she tried to ignore the fact that Cal's presence seemed to shrink the room by half. With every step she took, every turn she made, it seemed as though he was there, his scent was there, reminding her of all she couldn't have.

She picked up the paper, read the beautiful script. "She's gone shopping. It says here she'll be back by three." She passed the paper to him, watched him examine both sides, and then crumple it into a tiny ball.

His eyes fluttered closed and he leaned back against the paneled wall, his breathing ragged. "I was so worried. I'd thought he'd taken her."

Warning bells chimed in her head. "He who? Taken whom? Charley? Is she in some sort of danger?" Jack couldn't go through this again, another lunatic stalking a person she cared for. When would the nightmares end?

Slowly one eye opened, then another. "Her name is Charlotte."

"You're avoiding my questions. I have a right to know if she's in trouble." They'd add security, be more aware. She'd talk to Charley about not going out alone, of being more careful. Jack worried her lip. Perhaps they could hire someone . . . Jack knew of people who'd do anything for a price. Maybe they could scare this person away from Charley before anything horrible happened.

"Not *Charley* or *Chas* or even *Lottie*. Charlotte. She's a lady."

Her internal panic ebbed, her ire flaring. "She seems like a Charley to me. And she likes the name."

"It's not up to her." The pulse at the base of his throat jumped and strained against his skin with each word.

Hands on hips, she said, "Last I checked, she was a grown woman who could make up her own mind."

He dropped his head into his hands, muttered something about not having time to deal with this.

Curious, Jack stepped closer to him. "That's the second time you've said that."

Suspicion crept into his eyes. "What?"

"That's the second time you've said that you didn't have time. Why's that?"

He pushed away from the wall, his large frame edging closer to her; a tiger on the prowl. "I've no idea what you're talking about."

She swallowed as he came nearer. The accusation barely passed her parched lips: "You're lying."

Leaning over her, he grinned, the smile not even

close to reaching his eyes. "Add it to all my other sins."

He started for the door, stopped and faced her. "I'm not at all pleased by this sleeping arrangement. This isn't a good idea."

His tone rankled. "Why's that? Am I a bad influence?"

"Yes. No." He shook his head, then nodded. "Yes. Yes, you are. How is she to find a society husband with a name like Charley?"

Replacing her hands on her hips, she glared. "Maybe Charley doesn't want a society husband. Have you ever thought of that?"

He looked momentarily stunned, as though the idea had never crossed his mind.

"Can I offer you some advice, Cal? As a friend?"

He looked at her with those gray-green eyes that no longer looked lifeless. No, now they seemed full of vitality, of heat, of fire.

"Tell me, Jack, is that what we are?"

When he looked at her with such blatant fervor she could barely think two coherent thoughts. She took a step back, away from him, and bumped into Lou's armoire, the handles knocking against the wood in loud protest.

"Well?" he asked, advancing toward her.

She licked her lips. "Well, what?" Oh how she needed a sip of water. Her mouth had gone dryer than a ball of cotton. It seemed as though her throat was closing in, cutting off her air.

She let her gaze drop to the wooden floor. It was better than looking at him, at those eyes.

His thumb nudged her chin. Slowly she looked up, tried with all her might to avoid his impassioned gaze, and failed miserably.

Ribbons of warmth unfurled in her stomach at the touch of his callused finger, spreading languorous heat to her limbs. He spoke, his warm breath smelling slightly of coffee as it washed over her, lured her toward him, toward those full lips of his, those hooded, passionate eyes. "I asked," he said, "if we were friends?"

Cal stared down at Jack, saw the way she looked up at him. She might be angry with him, maybe even hate him, but her body, and perhaps her heart, had yet to accept that fact.

Her moist lips trembled as she said, "Friends?"

"Are we friends?" he asked, doing his best to ignore how easy it would be to pull her into his arms, kiss her senseless, get so lost in her that he'd forget his problems forever.

Tempting indeed.

Down the hall, a door slammed, and he saw the change in Jack as she heard it too.

Straightening, she snapped her mouth into a thin, solid line, ducked away from him, and hurried to the other side of the room.

The spell had been broken. Any hopes he fostered of gaining her forgiveness vanished like smoke on the wind.

She turned to face him after a moment of staring out the window. "I don't know if I can be friends with you."

Why was it that honesty so often hurt?

"Because of my cheating?"

Her long lashes fluttered, shuttering her deep blue eyes. How she fooled others at the poker table, he'd never know. Hers were the most expressive, articulate eyes he'd ever seen. Just looking at her told him all he needed to know.

And what he saw now was that he'd lost her forever.

"Why?" she asked. "Why cheat?"

He closed the distance between them in two long strides. He stroked the side of her face, felt her press her cheek into the palm of his hand. Looking deep into her eyes, he revealed more than he intended by saying, "Some things, Jack, are worth cheating for."

He couldn't go into it with her, tell her why it had to be done, so he kept quiet. She'd already forgotten about his slip earlier—when he'd voiced his fears about Daley Lombard aloud. He'd been wrong, thankfully, Daley hadn't come for Charlotte. Not yet. But how long did Cal have before he would?

Why cheat, she had asked. *Why?* Because he had no other option. Because his father had cheated and lost, and Charlotte now had to pay the price, unless Cal cheated too. And he would, to save his sister from a lifetime of misery.

Again, she ducked beneath his arm. "Am I supposed to understand that?"

He shrugged. This conversation was pointless. She wanted answers he couldn't give, and he wanted forgiveness without explaining why.

"How long has it been going on?" she pressed.

He wanted to confide in her, share his problems, but he kept silent. He'd gambled for years to pay for Charlotte's expensive schooling, but he had never resorted to cheating. Had never stooped so low. But now he had no choice.

"Does it matter?" he asked wearily, suddenly feeling as though the world sat on his shoulders, dragging him down.

Softly, she said, "It does to me."

It was those eyes of hers that prompted the truth from him. "Not long."

She folded her arms over her chest, the black fabric of her shirt stretching taut. "I believe you."

Anger rose up, burst forth out. "Why shouldn't you? I've never lied to you."

"How do I know?" Her voice cracked. "I thought I knew you, Cal."

He breathed in, held the air for a moment before releasing it in a soft whoosh. He turned on his heel and headed to the door without a backward glance.

The brass knob felt cool in his hand as he turned it. With all the integrity he could muster, he said, "You do know me, Jack. More than you could ever guess."

Chapter Six

Cal's words still echoed in Jack's head hours later as she led Minx toward the Searcy farm.

The five-year-old quarter horse belonged to the livery near the Landing and had become her favorite to ride over the past few months.

Jack leaned forward, patting the mare's neck as they rode toward the outskirts of River Glen. The tooled leather saddlebag fastened securely under her right thigh held what money she could round up, and she hoped that it was enough to appease old Gus Searcy. Surely he wouldn't turn down such a large deposit for his land? She couldn't bear to think about losing the ranch to someone else.

As she neared the land that would soon be hers, Jack couldn't help but smile. Wide, open, rolling meadows stretched as far as her eye could see, every now and then broken by a thick copse of trees and underbrush that would provide ample shade for her horses. She knew there to be several watering holes scattered about also. A pole and beam fence covered in barbwire looked near to falling over, but Jack could work on that. She'd do anything she had to do to make this work, anything to raise the rest of that money.

But not cheat. She'd do, and had done, many things that bordered on the immoral, but she'd never cheat.

You do know me, Jack. More than you could ever guess.

Try as she might, she couldn't prevent Cal's baleful tone from taunting her. Unintentionally, her hands tightened on the reins and Minx pulled her head hard to the right.

"Sorry, pretty girl," Jack murmured, letting loose the reins and allowing Minx to control the pace.

It wasn't so much *what* Cal had said but *how* he said it. Rough-edged, filled with the sorrow of a suffering man.

She tugged her hat down lower over her eyes as the road bent westward. Cal had sounded wounded, and his pain resonated inside her, sitting like an anchor in her stomach, making her doubt what she knew of him.

Setting aside what she had recently learned, she concentrated on the Cal she used to know. On his friendship with Matt, the years of loyalty. His generosity. After all, if it hadn't been for his loan a few months back, the *Amazing Grace* would probably be long since dismantled, her aging floorboards used as firewood. And Jack's family . . . her family would undoubtedly be destitute, living off the grace of others.

Minx's coat shimmered with each step she took, the sleek sable mane flying in a mesmerizing rhythm.

Cal had been a great friend to her too, accepting her, or so she thought, for who she was, her true self. He'd been the only man who'd ever done so.

Apparently he'd been a great actor.

Shaking her head, she forced herself to ignore all the negatives and focus on the positives. She forced herself to erase completely these past few days from her thoughts.

Who was Cal, really?

You do know me, Jack.

If it hadn't been for the tremendous pain in his voice when he spoke those words, she wouldn't let her doubts fester. As it was, she didn't know what to do, or what to make of Cal and his actions.

Before he'd come back, she would have bet everything she owned, including the shirt on her back, that he was a man of honor, of principles. Noble yet amazingly humble. He had that way about him. He'd drawn her to him from the first moment she looked into his eyes and thought she'd seen something . . . *special.*

Truly special.

Moisture burned her eyes. Furiously, she swiped at those damnable tears. She didn't want to cry for him. Or for what she had lost. It was senseless and altogether fruitless. Crying would not change what happened, what Cal had done, what he had said.

Nor would it change the fact that her heart still yearned for him, despite how he'd hurt her. Despite the fact that he didn't want her.

This was her own stupid, rash fault. They'd never professed anything to each other. Certainly not love. She and Cal had shared a friendship, one she let her mind build into something more. Something very real to her, but completely in her head. All this heartache she felt now . . . well, she had no one to blame but herself.

Dirt kicked up beneath Minx's hooves; the ground parched by the summer sun. Cicadas hummed from the tall grass and underbrush lining the road and birds serenaded her as her thoughts circled round and round.

Who was the real Cal? The noble, honorable man? The lying, cheating sneak?

Or could he be both? Was it possible to harbor two different personalities?

"Who is he, Minx?" she said aloud. Leaning forward, she rubbed the mare's long neck.

Straightening, she tried to make sense of it all. Of him.

"Okay, he cheated."

Minx snorted.

"Why? Money, right?" Money was the only motive for cheating. She'd thought it herself a moment ago.

She tipped her head to the side, stretching the stiff muscles in her neck. Thoughts, possibilities swirled. Her breath hitched as her mind landed on a notion so startling she nearly toppled out of the saddle.

It did make sense in an odd, roundabout way.

Could it be possible that Cal's honor and selfless nature led him to cheat?

You do know me, Jack.

Yes, she did. Maybe not all of him, but enough. Cal needed money. Desperately. So much so that he'd cheat to get it.

The only question that begged an answer now was *why?* Why when he seemed to be quite well-off? Charley's schooling had to cost a small fortune in itself.

She let her thoughts tumble inside out and upside down trying to come up with an explanation. And couldn't. There was only one way to find out if her conjectures were correct and that was to ask Cal. And hope he'd be truthful.

Searcy's small ranch house came into view and Jack frowned at the way the whole structure leaned just a bit to the left. Another thing to fix.

Oh what she wouldn't do to find land somewhere and start from scratch. Build her own house, board by board. Again, the vast plains and breathtaking hills of the Montana landscape came to mind. She almost wished she'd never seen the photographs in magazines of the lands to the west. Then she wouldn't still be clinging to a fruitless dream.

She pulled back on the reins and Minx slowed to a stop. This land would do just fine. It had its share of problems, but she'd be on top of them in no time at all. She was sure of it.

Besides, if she started to doubt, she'd never have the courage to fulfill this small portion of the dreams she harbored.

With a gentle nudge, she guided Minx down the dirt road dappled with sunlight by the outstretched branches of old maple trees standing guard on each side of her.

Perspiration beaded on the back of her neck, sliding down her spine. Her braid thumped her back steadily as she rode along.

Two stone-stacked cairns marked the long narrow lane leading to the house. The long grass hung limp and had turned brown. Dandelions offered splashes of color as evergreens threw long shadows down the path.

As the house came into sight, Jack pulled back gently on the reins, slowing Minx. Paint peeled from the clapboards and weeds sprouted from around the foundation of the structure. A crooked crab tree offered little shade for the front porch.

It needed work, she'd be the first to admit that, but there was no harder worker than she. Given time she'd make this place shine.

The front door swung open as she dismounted, and

old Gus Searcy came out on the rickety front porch, his plaid shirt stretched taut over his distended belly. Red suspenders held up a pair of denim trousers that needed to be let out at the cuffs. Black stockings slouched at his ankles. There was a hole in the toe of one boot.

"Miss Parker, pleasure to be seein' you again." He swiped a handkerchief across his wrinkled forehead as he came down two steps to greet her.

"Hello, Mr. Searcy."

"I be takin' it you've raised the funds you need?"

Wishing she'd been born with just an ounce of the charm Lou possessed, she smiled. She'd even take Alex's forthright, stubborn demeanor right about now as she pulled off her riding gloves.

She couldn't leave this farm without Mr. Searcy's agreement to sell it to her. Raising her own horses was all she'd wanted since she was old enough to sit upright in a saddle. She had to have this land.

"Not exactly," she said, looking down at him. He was at least a head shorter.

"Now, Miss Parker, you know I be needin' that money soon. I've been gettin' offers that sound mighty temptin'."

Panic swirled in her stomach. "I'm sure you have, Mr. Searcy, but my offer is quite generous." Minx stamped her hoof as if in complete agreement.

"Indeed it is. But I ain't seen nothin' to show by it."

Jack swallowed over her nervousness. "I've brought you a deposit." Unbuckling the saddlebag, she hoped the money was enough. Enough for him to hold off on other offers, at least until the end of the month.

Two thick envelopes weighed heavily in her hand. She turned to him. "Fifteen hundred dollars. I should have the other half by the end of the month, as we agreed before."

His narrow eyes went wide. A smile bloomed. "I had my doubts, girl, I must say. But this," he held up the envelope, "this is proof I be wrong."

"Will you hold off on accepting other offers as we agreed?"

Using his thumb, he counted off bills.

"Mr. Searcy? Is it a deal?" Mentally, she winced. Did he hear that tinge of panic?

"Wha—Sure, sure."

"If for some reason I can't raise the rest of the money, I'll of course want my money refunded, minus five hundred dollars for your trouble."

He went on counting, his eyes going wider and wider. Minx snorted behind her, stamped her hoofs.

"Is that acceptable? Mr. Searcy?"

He opened the other envelope, waved her away. "Refund. Yes, indeed."

She steeled her shoulders, lifted her chin. "I'd like our agreement written down, Mr. Searcy. Signed by both of us."

He finally looked up at her, his cheeks jiggling with the movement. "Sure, sure. Come on in and we'll make somethin' up."

Jack tethered Minx to the porch, hoping the wood would hold. A smile tugged on her lips as she followed Mr. Searcy into the house, the excitement that this would all be hers nearly making her laugh aloud with happiness.

Everything she'd always wanted lay in her grasp. Almost everything. She wanted the truth from Cal, not only about his gambling, but about Charley too. Those comments he'd made about Charley being taken hadn't been forgotten. Not at all. She'd get her answers from him. She'd make sure of it.

Pushing all thoughts of Cal out of her mind, she stepped over the threshold of the home that would soon be hers. And even lingering thoughts of Cal and his many deceptions couldn't tarnish this moment.

Charlotte was avoiding him. He was avoiding Jack. And if this pain in his head lasted another blasted day he would seriously consider weighting his ankles and tossing himself overboard, Cal thought grimly.

If he had any sense left he'd just head to the Maybury and get lost in the cards. Forget about everything. Everyone. Including Jack Parker.

He didn't think he could stand looking into her soulful eyes and seeing disappointment aimed his way once more. Her disapproval was like a knife to the gut.

Lying on his bed, a cool cloth covering his eyes, he tried not to think about how he'd manage to avoid Jack for another two weeks. But maybe God's grace would shine on him and she'd want to avoid him too.

He groaned. The thought that she would purposely avoid him caused the pain in his head to intensify. He squeezed his eyes tightly, fighting off the ache.

Maybe it was time to see a doctor. He'd never much been one for medicine, but he could take only so much. Or maybe he'd try one of those ridiculous powders he'd seen at the drug store. He was that desperate. The pain was getting to the point where banging his head against the wall sounded enticing.

Flinging the cloth off his face, he blinked at the low lamplight. A wave of nausea came and went as he sat up. Dragging a hand over his eye, Jack's image appeared.

He'd been a fool.

A fool to think that he could simply discard his feelings for her. While back on the Double C, he'd tried his best to forget her. And he could. For a while. Until he closed his eyes at night and dreamed of her eyes, the curve of her cheeks, the tilt of her chin. Until he woke up in the morning longing to find her by his side, that mischievous sparkle in her eye, her contagious laughter warming him.

Even if he were in her good graces, he had nothing to offer her, he reminded himself. What money he had was earmarked for Charlotte. The Double C didn't belong to him, so he couldn't even offer her the ranch she'd said she always wanted. There was that, too. How many times had she told him of her dreams to raise horses on the vast Montana prairies? To live off the land, be one with nature? That just wasn't him. He was a city boy at heart, despite being raised on a ranch. Or maybe because of it.

Yet, if given half the chance, he'd go back to that miserable life. Of feeding chickens at dawn, checking on the herd long after dusk. Falling into bed half asleep and waking only to think of when he'd get the chance to sleep again. He'd go back to all of it. If it meant he could be with Jack forever. In a heartbeat he'd go back.

This wasn't even his mess. It was his father's. If it hadn't been for Hoyt McQue, Cal would have everything he wanted.

He splashed cold water on his face and tucked in his shirt. He needed to get off this boat for a while. Leave his demons behind. For even though it was his father's mess, he was the one who had to clean it up. Hadn't it always been that way?

Yanking open the door, he stopped short. Charlotte stood in the hallway, her hand poised to knock.

"I'm glad you're here," she said.

His eyes widened. "What are you wearing?"

Her gaze dropped, then raised, a twinkle in her eye. "Pants. Don't you like them?" She spun in a small circle, her arms outstretched.

He pulled a hand over his face, feeling a day's worth of stubble. "No."

Her mouth hardened. "That's too bad." She pushed past him, settled herself in the chair next to his bed.

Slowly, he closed the door. Pain pulsated behind his eyes. It was true he'd been looking for her for hours, but now that she was here he didn't have the wherewithal to get into it with her. She needed a lecture on propriety desperately, but he just didn't have the *stamina* at the moment to deliver it.

Lines creased her forehead as she frowned. "Can I ask you something?"

He let out a ragged sigh, leaned against the door. "What?"

Her foot tapped, and lo and behold, she was wearing cowboy boots. He closed his eyes. Lord help him.

"I thought you were fond of Jack."

Perhaps he'd weight his ankles right this minute and hurl himself out his window. "That's not a question."

"I mean," she said, ignoring him, "you always spoke of her with such high regard, in your letters to me at school, and then later, when we were at the Double C."

He spoke through clenched teeth. "Still not a question."

Her large green eyes, so like their father's shown with emotion, determination. He drew in a fortifying breath in preparation of an impending attack.

"Don't you like her anymore?"

The knife in his gut twisted. "It's none of your concern, Charlotte."

"But it is."

"No, it's not."

Standing, she placed her hands on her hips. "The way you spoke of her made me think . . ."

She lifted her chin. Was that another trait she'd adopted from Jack or had he never realized how stubborn his sister was?

". . . it made me think that you loved her."

Heaven above, he needed to sit down. Pain arced out like lightning across his forehead, behind his eyes. Knowing he had to say something—anything—to appease her, he tightly said, "Jack—Well, Jack . . ." He clenched his fists. "She's amazing," he said with a ragged sigh.

Charlotte stamped her foot. "Then why?" she cried out.

At her sudden outburst, he straightened. "Why what?"

"Why don't you see that we're similar, Jack and I? Why can't you see that I want to lead my own life, wear clothes *I* pick, run the Double C *my* way, marry a man *I* choose? If you think *she's* so amazing," her voice caught, "why can't you see that *I'm* amazing too?"

Realization hit him like a thump on the head. In all the years he'd spent trying to give Charlotte the best, mold her into what their mother had been, that society belle who'd had it all, he'd never seen what he'd been doing to her: killing her spirit.

He crossed the room, tugged her into his arms. "You are amazing. I'm sorry I've never told you so before." He drew back, but kept hold of her. "I want what's best for you, is all."

Her lower lip quivered. "Don't you think I know what's best for me?"

He shook his head. "As a man I see things differently."

Pulling away, she said, "Well, if that's not the most bigoted thing I've ever heard."

Their childhood had been miserable, filled with anger, yelling, and sadness. He'd wanted to make it up to her, atone for the past by offering her the foundations for a happy future. "It's true. I wanted you to have a good life, that's all. Mother was so restless living on the ranch. She was so much happier living in Louisville where she had friends to call on, where there were parties every night, where she belonged."

She touched his arm. "I'm not Mother."

He grabbed her hands. "Don't you see? Ranch life killed her. It took the vitality right out of her eyes and eventually stole her life."

Charlotte closed her eyes for a moment. When she opened them, he saw tears shining. "No, she wasn't happy. She thought she'd marry Father and convert him to something he wasn't. But she loved him and she stayed."

"Against her will."

Long strands of golden hair flew out as Charlotte shook her head. "No. She was there because she loved him."

"And look what it did for her!" He turned away. "You need to find a good man, Charlotte. One who listens to what you want, what you need, who will know instinctively what will make you happy."

She looked down at her toes. "I don't need a man to be happy, Cal. I can do that on my own. I want a man who loves me. Me. Not someone I'm pretending to be to make others happy."

"But—" He broke off, Jack's earlier comment ringing in his head.

Maybe Charley doesn't want a society husband. Have you ever thought of that?

He looked at his little sister. No longer was she the little mite who'd follow him from place to place, annoying him with endless questions. She was a grown woman, even if he didn't want to think of her that way.

Clearing his throat, he said, "Is there someone, Charlotte?"

"Someone who?"

"Someone you love? You speak as if you have someone in mind."

"No." She looked away.

Her answer came just a bit too quickly for him to believe her. What was she hiding? Or rather, whom?

Before he could ask, she said, "I want to live life for myself. Make my own choices, decisions. Learn from my own mistakes." She held out her hands, palm up. "I wanted to do this long before I ever heard Jack Parker's name, so don't blame her. Jack just gave me the confidence in myself to finally be the person *I* want to be."

"You barely know her."

"I know enough. She has a way about her. Self-assurance, I suppose."

He turned away from her and looked out the window. The moon hovered between low hanging clouds; specks of the city lights glowed like stars. "Jack's not had an easy time of it. Did she tell you?"

"No."

"Rumors, whispers, hurtful remarks."

He heard rustling behind him. "She turned out well."

How did he argue with that? It was true. Jack did turn out well. Quite well. She was the most extraordinary woman he'd ever known.

"Even still," he said.

He heard the turn of the doorknob, then turned to find Charlotte looking at him somberly, the door open. "I wouldn't worry about Jack, Cal. After all, she has you." Her eyebrows shot up. "I hope you haven't ruined your relationship with her."

The door closed behind her. Cal rocked on his heels, leaned his aching head against the windowpane. Despite his best judgment, he hoped he hadn't either.

Chapter Seven

A stiff warm breeze blew up from the south, loosening Jack's tight braid. Soft tendrils of hair blew across her face, clinging to her moist lips. She pushed the wayward locks behind her ears as she stared out of the darkened river waiting for Cal to return.

Thick heavy clouds hung low, darkening the midnight sky. Flickering gaslight from a bronze sconce threw long shadows across the wooden planks, creating eerie pockets along the deck where Jack wouldn't even be able to see her hand in front of her face.

Lifting her chin, she raised her gaze to the sky, enjoying the wind on her face. Nearly midnight and all was quiet on the boat and quieter still on the Landing. Gentle currents lapped at the shallow hull of the steamer.

Jack leaned against the wooden railing enclosing the main deck, bracing her weight on her elbows. She propped her chin in her hands.

What was she going to say to him? She had the squirrelly feeling that he wasn't going to be open and forthright with her. He hadn't been so far.

A spark of worry sank like a leaded ball to the hollow of her stomach. Was Charley in danger?

I'd thought he'd taken her.

Cal had been worried. He'd admitted so before he caught himself and returned to being the tight-lipped, stubborn man he was.

She'd seen Charley earlier that evening but hadn't wanted to discuss Charley's relationship with Cal. Not yet. Maybe not ever. It wasn't her place. However, she wasn't above a little subtle prying to get information. If she had to.

Sighing, she rolled her tension filled shoulders. She had been determined to speak with Cal tonight, but as the night deepened the more tired she became.

It had been a long day, what with the encounter with Cal that morning and then the meeting with Mr. Searcy.

She yawned wide, her tired eyes begging for sleep. As she walked a bit to stretch her legs, her gaze wandered to the empty Landing.

Where was he?

Decking creaked beneath her weight and she nearly laughed aloud at the ridiculous question. She knew where he was: gambling.

Bravely, she had ventured into the Maybury earlier, ready to face Wheezy and his accusations, but all had been quiet—much to her relief. Fifteen hundred additional dollars and the Searcy land would be hers. Actually, $1315.00 and the land would be hers— thanks to the winnings she'd accumulated earlier.

A frown tugged on her lips as another yawn escaped. If she continued to accrue such small amounts she'd never meet Mr. Searcy's deadline. There had to be another way.

Yawning again, she stretched her arms high above

her head. Cal had been deeply entrenched in a poker game when she'd left. She hadn't lingered to see if he was cheating. She didn't want to know.

That had been nearly two hours ago. The wind rattled at the *Amazing Grace's* weathered boards, rocking the boat. To the south, lightning illuminated the Kentucky horizon.

She listened for thunder but heard none. However, a strong sulfur scent teased the air, promising some much needed rain.

A few minutes more, she told herself. That's all she'd allow. Already her eyelids hung heavy.

A long noiseless yawn brought tears of exhaustion to her eyes.

"It's past your bedtime, Jack."

Jack spun, grabbing her heart as it threatened to beat its way right out of her chest. Cal lurked in the shadows near the doors leading inside.

Quickly, she found her voice. "I didn't see you there."

"I don't suppose you did."

Folding her arms over her chest, she wasn't entirely sure what to make of his lazy, rough tone. How long had he been watching her?

She lifted her chin. "I've been waiting for you."

"Have you now?"

Leaning back, she let the railing support her weight. There was something, deep, dark, and promising in his voice. Something she longed for, yet knew was forbidden.

Waiting for him had been a bad idea.

Swallowing a thick lump in her throat, she fought through the fogginess in her head for an excuse to abruptly leave. Somewhere deep down warning bells sounded. Staying here with him would only lead to other things . . . things best left unexplored. That lazy, languorous tone in his voice told her all she needed to know. A quick retreat was definitely in order. "I, er, I think I'll head to bed."

He pushed away from the wall, but remained in the shadows. "Why the rush?"

Edging slowly toward the double doors, she said, "I just th—I mean, I don't thi—" Her heart kicked against her breastbone. She gave up on trying to come up with something clever. "I need to go."

With a soft chuckle, he stepped out of the shadows, blocking her escape. The low burning gas lamp threw soft light across his face.

Jack gasped. Without thinking, she stepped forward to touch the swollen raised skin around his eye. "What happened?"

He captured her hand and her mouth went dry. Her head snapped up and she found him looking at her with such immense tenderness that what was left of her broken heart shattered.

"Stay," he whispered, his breath caressing her cheek. "Just for a minute."

"I—" Desperately, she looked around. For what, she didn't know. A means of escape? Or a place to hide away from prying eyes?

"Please."

Moisture stung at her eyes at the startling realization that she would do anything for him. Even after all she'd learned of him in the last few days—or maybe because of it. She wasn't sure, but knew she couldn't leave him. Not now at any rate.

Soon enough she'd be gone and he'd be out of her life. Oh, she'd probably see him on occasion, and perhaps they'd say hello and query the other's well being, but she knew without a doubt that this night would never be spoken of again. For that she was grateful.

"O—okay."

Breathing deep, he pressed her palm to his stubble-roughened cheek, tipped his head, and closed his eyes.

His fingers held tightly onto her wrist, preventing her from leaving, as though he couldn't trust her. Surely he knew that when she gave her word she meant it. She'd yet to go back on a promise, to go back on her word, and she couldn't foresee a day when she would. Her integrity was *that* important to her.

Slowly, she let her thumb glide over the enticing stubble on his chin. Knowing she shouldn't be so bold, she continued anyway. She savored the feel of him, and this new side of Cal, this vulnerability.

"What happened?" she whispered again, though she could guess. Someone had caught him cheating, no doubt. In which case, he was lucky to escape with only a bruised eye.

His chest rumbled under her hand as he said, "Does it matter?"

The lamp flickered. Under her palm his heart beat fast and furious. She supposed not. "Does it hurt?"

Long-lashed eyes flickered open. He smiled. "Only when I smile."

She grinned up at him. "Then don't."

The dark night concealed his quicksilver green eyes, but added depth to the look he gave her. Her breath caught, then released. She couldn't tear her gaze from those eyes of his, from the warmth and intensity she saw there.

Her thumb swept over the plane of his cheek in mesmerizing rhythm as she continued to stare, lamp-light flickered in the wind and thunder rumbled in the distance.

Ever so slowly, his head inched lower. A knot of something uninhibited and wild unwound in her stomach as she lifted her lips to meet his.

Cal pressed her to him, their two hearts now beating as one. His thumb caressed a spot on the back of her neck, sending a shiver down her spine.

Slowly, oh so slowly, she watched as his head lowered. For a moment, just as his lips hovered so near to her own, a feather light touch against her sensitive skin, she forgot to breathe. Her heart stopped, then flared to life as his lips touched gently against her own.

She fell into the kiss without bracing her heart for the pain it would later feel. Her hand snaked up, curving around the back of his neck. Thick, coarse hair met her touch, and she sank her fingers in deeper, pulling his head closer to hers.

Behind her closed eyes, lights danced as her heart leapt with the knowledge that this was where she belonged. In this man's arms. His lips on her own.

The kiss deepened, and she met the challenge with the pleasure of knowing he was as equally affected as she. The violent beating of his heart against her chest betrayed his inner emotions.

Lost in his touch, she didn't care that this might be wrong. All she knew was that nothing in her life had ever felt so right.

Jack leaned into him, trying to capture something she couldn't identify. Something she wanted more than anything at that moment. Something she needed desperately.

This feeling of desperation shocked her back to her senses. She jumped back, her hand flying to her lips as she stared up at him, barely able to breathe. Words failed her as she saw the hurt in the way his shoulders slumped, the downward tilt of his chin.

Swallowing hard, and fighting an annoying quiver in her legs, she reached her hand out to touch him, to console him, to ease his pain, but then pulled it back. Slowly, he straightened, looking everywhere but at her. There was nothing she wanted more than to fall into his arms and have him kiss her the whole night long, but she knew it was a fantasy best left unsaid.

There was too much between them, too many hurtful words, too many obstacles. Losing her heart to him had been a painful mistake. She wouldn't let it happen again. "We shouldn't."

He pulled a hand over his face. "I know."

His agreement tightened that infernal knot in her chest. Emotion clogged her throat.

Shaking his head, he walked to the railing and peered over. "You should go in. It's getting cold out here."

Even as he said it, goose bumps covered her arms. Tucking a wind-tussled lock of hair behind her ear, she watched Cal as he rocked back and forth, looking out over the dark river.

Sleep was the last thing on her mind. All drowsiness she had felt earlier vanished the moment he had stepped from the shadows, touched his lips to hers.

The deck groaned as she stepped toward him. Slowly, she lifted her hand to touch his arm.

He jerked away from her. "Go away, Jack."

Her steely countenance prevented her from turning tail and running. "No."

Lightning arced in the southern sky as he spun toward her. Frantically, he gestured between them. "This won't work. This . . . whatever this is between us. We both know that. So just go and let me be."

Folding her arms across her chest for warmth, she stared at him. "Please tell me what's going on. I see the pain in your eyes, hear the hurt in your voice. Please, tell me."

"There's nothing to share."

"You're lying."

His long fingers curled around the wooden railing. "So what if I am?"

"Maybe I can help."

"Help?" His bark of laughter sounded loud and harsh in the quiet night. "I don't think so."

"Does it have to do with Charley?" Tentatively, she stepped nearer to him, heard his deep, angry breaths. "With what you said earlier about the man taking her?"

"Just let it be, Jack."

Reaching up, she tugged on his chin, making him look down at her. "I can't."

"Why not?"

She couldn't put words to the way she was feeling. All she knew was that she had to help him, help take away that pain in his eyes.

Head tipped to the side, she shrugged. "I care."

"Well, don't." He turned to go.

She grabbed his sleeve. He stopped but didn't face her. "Earlier," she said, "when you said that I knew you more than I could guess . . . I do know you, Cal."

Thunder clapped overhead. She walked around him to face him. Night shadowed his eyes but couldn't hide his tortured expression. "Hide as you might behind that cranky attitude and foolhardy stubbornness, I do know you." She took his hands. "Maybe it took me just a bit to see past the devil-may-care personality you've adopted since your return, but the Cal I knew is still in there."

"Have you forgotten my cheating?" he said bitterly.

"Your cheating is what eventually made me realize how mistaken I had been. It showed me an honorable man who's at his wit's end. A man who would never even think about cheating unless he had no other choice. What I want to know is why. What happened in Louisville that's changed you so much? Is someone threatening you?"

With a tug, he pulled his hands from hers. Pushing his fingers through his unruly hair, he said, "It's none of your concern, Jack."

She played her trump card. "Maybe I should ask Charley."

"No! Leave Charley out of this."

Rubbing away the goose bumps on her arms, she stared at him, wondering if he realized he'd just given her one of the answers she had been looking for. Whatever he was going through had to do with Charley.

Pushing his fists against his forehead, he groaned. "You can't help. No one can help. Just stay out of it."

"I can't. I'm worried about you. This," she gently traced the angry bruise around his eye, "justifies my fears."

He sighed. "What will allay them, Jack? What can I possibly say, or do, to appease you?"

There were so many things she wanted, but one more than all the rest. "Stop cheating. It seems to me it's hurting you as much as anyone."

"I—"

She held up a hand. "Do not tell me you can't. You can. Any gambling you need to do, you can do fairly."

He drew his hand down his face and stared at her for a long moment. "As I said before, some things, Jack, are worth cheating for."

"What about me?" she said softly.

"What about you?"

"Am I worth *not* cheating for?"

"Lord above," he murmured.

"Am I, Cal? Do you care nothing for me?"

He took hold of her shoulders, pulling her close to him. "You mean everyt—" He took a shuddering breath. "I care for you, Jack. I truly do."

"Then promise me."

He let go of her, threw his head back, and stared up at the cloudy night. After a long moment, he looked back at her. "I promise."

Softly, she said, "Thank you."

"Now you have to do something for me."

The hard tone of his voice left her feeling cold. "What?"

"Charley and I will be gone in two weeks' time, until then please just stay away from me. I do not want to start something with you that I know I cannot finish. So, please."

It took Jack a moment to digest what he had said. "You're leaving?" Her stomach somersaulted; moisture stung her eyes.

Two long strides took Cal to the double doors leading inside. "Yes. Charlotte and I will remain in Louisville after we make the trip down."

"W—why?"

"I'm going to help run the Double C."

Grateful the cover of darkness hid the tears in her eyes, she swallowed a lump in her throat. Leaving? Forever? No occasional meetings, no return to the friendly banter they used to share. "But you hate ranching."

"I know."

"Then why go?" Dear heavens, she sounded like a

whiny child. Where was that iron backbone people always accused her of having when she needed it?

"Sometimes, Jack, we have to do things we don't want to do . . . things that are for the best. For everyone." He pulled open the door. His voice softened. "Like walking away from you tonight." Taking backward steps, he gazed at her for a long, agonizing minute before disappearing down the corridor.

Feeling as though her insides were twisting into knots, Jack crumpled to the deck. She pulled her knees tight to her chest, giving in to the torrent of tears.

Cal was leaving.

Somehow she'd thought that if she could help him with whatever troubles he had, perhaps then . . . Perhaps they'd be able to be together. Leave the past behind them and move forward together. A silly fantasy if she admitted the truth to herself. Ranching would be a noose around his neck, whether it was on the Double C or on her spread.

She swiped at the tears rolling down her cheeks, even though they were quickly replaced. It was high time she stopped dreaming and started living. Stop worrying about Cal and focus on herself.

The ache at the core of her being told her it wasn't going to be easy. But she would manage. She always had.

Letting the tears flow freely, she jumped as thunder clapped overhead. The skies didn't even have the decency to rain.

Chapter Eight

It had been nearly two weeks since Cal had told Jack to stay away and he'd regretted the words every day since. He'd asked her to leave him be, yet he yearned to have her near. He was nothing but a coward where she was concerned.

The memory of her lips haunted him. It didn't take much to remind him of the kiss they'd shared. The night's darkness, a strong breeze, the musty scent of the river. His every sense came alive, remembering, each time the boat swayed just so, the lamplight flickered. The taste of her lips came back to him, taunting him.

He sighed. If kissing her had been an error on his part, he wanted to live a life full of mistakes. Nothing compared to the way she made him feel. The touch of her hand on his neck, the look in her eyes. It almost made him feel worthy—of her, of life.

Almost.

He tacked a colored ribbon to the wall of the ballroom. Shaking his head, he took a long look at the decorations he'd already hung. Alex and her crazy ideas.

A masquerade ball of all things. Eminently glad he already had plans for tomorrow night, he didn't mind doing this bit of effortless work for Alex. It made it easier to look her in the eye when he told her he wasn't going to be sticking around for the ball.

Tomorrow night a high stakes poker game that was the key to his future was being held at O'Malley's Pub. If he lost, he risked losing Charley and that wasn't an option. He'd kill Daley Lombard before he'd let the lily-livered man marry his sister.

Swallowing hard, he wished he hadn't made that promise to Jack not to cheat. At that point, standing in the darkened night, her taste still on his lips, he'd have lassoed the moon and given it to her if she'd asked. Now, however, he was beginning to doubt his playing abilities. But he was determined to keep his promise to Jack. She deserved that much. He'd push aside his worries for now. He had time enough to stew about the money he still needed later.

"A little to the left, and down a bit," Alex said from behind him.

Tugging the tack from the plaster, he positioned it lower. "Here?"

"More to the right."

"Here?"

"Up some."

He pushed the tack into the same hole he'd just removed it from. "How's that?"

"Perfect. Thanks, Cal."

Cal sent silent sympathies to her husband, Matt, who was busy decorating the other side of the room as Alex walked toward him.

The ladder scraped the inlaid wood floor as he re-positioned himself under a beam and unfurled more ribbon. He looked around wishing Jack was here—she would make this tedious work fun.

He didn't blame Jack for escaping every day. Not only did Alex strive for perfection, but her to-do list was a fathom long. Unfortunately, he couldn't fool himself. Jack wasn't avoiding the *Amazing Grace* because of Alex, but because he'd asked her to stay away. And even if she had mind to ignore his request, he doubted she'd come calling.

Because of that kiss. The one he could still taste. The one he wanted to finish.

Wooden rungs protested his weight. With more force than necessary, he drove a tack into the wall, curling ribbon around it.

What had possessed him to kiss her in the first place? If anything, it only added to his problems. It was best they avoided each other. After all, he was leaving soon. No need to start something that couldn't be finished and end up hurting them both. This was why he requested she stay away.

Yet he couldn't help wanting her near.

Matt once accused him of mooning after Jack, back when he'd first met her and had been captivated by her charm. He felt that way now, like he was mooning. It was downright pathetic, but despite telling himself to cease and desist with the unwanted emotion, it continued to plague him.

Coming down off the ladder, he turned to find Charley—darned if the name didn't fit her—talking with Alex.

Charley hadn't been herself since they'd come up from Louisville. Try as she might to hide her sadness behind quick smiles and longwinded, one-sided conversations, he saw the pain in her eyes.

Was it possible she knew about Daley Lombard's

debtor's note? He shook his head. Charlotte was too opinionated to keep quiet if she did know.

Tossing the ribbons down, he watched as Charley pulled some sort of garment from a package. Making his way over to her, he overheard Charley ask about the mail.

"Expecting a letter?" he asked.

Charley jumped, laughed nervously. "Me? No."

Her gaze shot everywhere from the floor to the high ceiling, but she wouldn't look him in the eye.

She was lying.

Again.

Sighing, he let the matter drop. For now. He supposed everyone had his or her own secrets. His gaze fell to the package in her hands. "What's that?"

Alex tried to hide a smile behind her long fingers. Curious, he looked between the two of them. "Well?"

Charley cleared her throat. "Your costume."

"My what?"

"I, er," Alex looked around. "I think I hear Matt calling my name."

His gaze narrowed on Alex's heart-shaped face and she winked at him. With his jaw dropped, he watched her scurry away. He turned to his sister. "My what?"

"Your eye looks so much better, almost healed. One would have to look close to see that it had been blackened at all. You never did tell me how it became bruised."

He stood firm. "I will not be waylaid by your tactics, Charley. Now, I will repeat myself just once more. My *what*?"

Charley looked up at him, all gooey smiles and fluttering lashes. "Your costume," she said, brightly. "For the ball."

"I am not going to the ball, Charley."

Her lower lip jutted. "You said you would."

"Never. I would never have said so."

"Well, I thought I heard you say differently."

Again she wouldn't look at him. One day soon he was going to have to speak to her about her lies.

"I didn't. I'm not going."

"Just look," she said, tugging a bright swath of fabric form the package. "It's Napoleon."

His head started to ache. He'd finally given in and gone to see a doctor. Tension, the man had said. He suggested Cal decrease his amount of stress. The fool. If he could do that, he wouldn't have been there. He'd just have to soldier on and bear the pain. As soon as this whole Lombard matter was resolved, he was sure it would ease.

"Napoleon! He wasn't bigger than a blade of wheat grass."

From the box at her feet, Charley pulled out a three cornered hat, teetered on her tiptoes, and set it on his head.

He glared. "No."

"You look smashing. Everyone will think so," she added, her eyes lighting up. "And those daggers flying from your eyes will be hidden by this." She pressed a mask into his hand.

"No."

She stomped her foot. "Please?"

When she looked at him that way it was tough to deny her anything, but sometimes he had to stand strong against her wily, sisterly ways. "No."

"You have to go. I won't know anyone there. Who will dance with me?"

"Matt."

"He'll be too busy mooning over Alex. She's going as a fairy godmother."

"I'm sorry, Charlotte, but no."

She looked up at him with those moon-pie eyes. Fluttered her lashes. Pouted.

He needed a drink.

Her hands clasped together, prayer-like, and she blinked up at him.

Absolutely not. No, no, no.

"Please, Cal? It would mean so much to me. I might even forgive you for making me come up here. You know as well as I do that I would have been perfectly fine staying with Grogan on the ranch. After all, there's so much to be done this time of year. Surely you must know that. Going to this ball as my escort is your brotherly duty, one I might point out you've neglected during my years at Mrs. Garrison's Fini—"

"Enough!" He couldn't take anymore of her jabbering. Lord help the man she married.

Hope sprang to her eyes. "You'll go?"

Pain pounded inside his skull. He hadn't been swayed by her theatrics until she hit on his weakness: his guilt at not being there for her while she grew up. Even recognizing her manipulation for what it was did little to ease the sting of the comment. The least he could do was make an appearance at the ball. He'd still have time to make it to his poker game. That is if Jack wasn't around. She had a tendency to sidetrack his thoughts. "Will Jack be attending?"

Charley shook her head. "No."

Good. That's just how he wanted it. Besides, he'd never live it down if she saw him in the Napoleon costume.

Charley continued on. "She said she'd rather jump off the stacks with flour bags weighting her ankles."

He knew the feeling. "I'll go."

He caught hold of her as she jumped all around, clapping her hands. "I won't be staying long."

"Long enough." She gathered up her packages.

"Long enough for what?"

"Hmmm?"

"Long enough for what, Charlotte?"

"I do so like it better when you call me Charley."

"Long enough for what?" he ground out through clenched teeth, suspicion flaring white-hot.

"I've got to get these pressed." She hurried toward the door. "We'll talk about it at dinner."

Suspicion turned to full-fledged dread. She knew darn well that, like every other night, he wouldn't be at dinner. He had a date with a poker table.

The chair Jack sat in had a loose cane that persisted in jabbing her whenever she shifted in the slightest direction.

Not that she was a fidgeter by nature, but certain circumstances set her feet twitching. Such as sitting in a bank, asking for a loan. Especially when the bank belonged to one Leona Mason, formerly Leona Farrell, who a mere two months ago despised Jack and her sisters.

Were those old feelings so easily overlooked as she'd have everyone believe? Or did they lurk beneath a phony facade, just waiting for a chance to rear up, strike out?

A set of half-glasses perched on the edge of Mrs. Mason's bulbous nose as she skimmed the loan papers Jack had so meticulously filled out.

"The Searcy land is a good investment, Miss Parker."

Nervous butterflies flitted here and there inside her stomach. "It's just what I've been looking for." She tapped her hat against her leg as Mrs. Mason continued to read. "I just need eight hundred more."

She'd manage to accrue just five hundred during the past two weeks. Not nearly enough.

Nodding, Mrs. Mason put the papers down and set her spectacles on the desk. "I'd love to loan you the money, Miss Parker—"

"Jack."

"Jack. However, I have a problem."

Jack's booted toe tapped. That infernal cane continued to poke her spine. "Problem?"

"Collateral."

"I don't have any."

"Yes, I know. That's the problem."

Gnawing her lip, Jack tried to think of something, anything.

"You do own one third of the *Amazing Grace,* correct?"

Her nervous stomach sank like lead to her toes. "I do."

"You could use that as collateral."

Jack swallowed. "And if I failed to repay the loan?"

"Then the bank would own one third of the *Amazing Grace.*"

Nausea roiled. The *bank.* Since Mrs. Mason owned the bank that meant the *Amazing Grace* would fall into her hands. It was unthinkable. Not that Jack planned on failing, but the risk was too great.

"I don't think so." Her fingers sought the brim of her hat, picked at the edge.

"In that case, perhaps someone to co-sign the loan for you? Someone with the money to back their name?"

Jack knew that her brother-in-law, John Hewitt, had

come from wealth and now used his family's money to support charities. Of which she didn't qualify.

Weakly, she said, "No."

"Your sisters, perhaps?"

"Mrs. Mason, I really wanted to do this on my own. My sisters do not even know of my plans."

"I see."

Jack jumped to her feet. "I'm afraid you don't."

Her deadline was in two days' time. There was simply no way to get that amount of money before then. Despite how hard she'd tried this past week, the poker tables had not been kind to her.

Setting her hat on her head, she held her hand out to Mrs. Mason.

"I'm sorry, Jack. But if I bent the rules for you . . ."

"I understand. Truly, I do."

In all honesty, she did. Pushing the door to the bank open, she stepped out into the blazing sun.

She could have that money if she swallowed her pride and asked her sisters for help, but that wasn't an option she'd dared consider. This was something she wanted to do on her own. All on her own.

But how?

Well after midnight, Jack pushed open the door to her room. She'd been out walking the river's edge for hours, trying to come up with some way to earn eight hundred dollars in two days' time. Perhaps she could ask Mr. Searcy for an extension? Perhaps she'd consider trying if only he hadn't made her deadline abundantly clear. But he'd been adamant. The end of the month and no longer.

A slash of light cut across Charley's bed. A long twist of blonde hair curled against the pillow, but a thin cotton sheet had been pulled up over her face.

Jack tiptoed in, trying not to make a sound, though she didn't know why. More often than not, Charley merely pretended to sleep.

As she undressed, Jack thought about how for so long she'd yearned for her life to be different. Her childhood had been anything but typical. Growing up with a father who believed females had every right that males did had been rather interesting.

The freedom suited her. She loved the clothes she was able to wear, the atypical education she had acquired. Yet as she grew, she realized something was missing. Some element she hadn't been able to name, and if pressed, still couldn't.

Buying land of her own came close to satisfying that emptiness. And being with Cal . . . He seemed to fulfill her like nothing else. To think of them together, married, with babies and love and laughter caused a yearning so strong it brought tears to her eyes.

Running a brush through her hair, she let her lids drift closed, and thought back to the kiss they'd shared nearly a week ago. Knees weak, she sat on the edge of her bed, the soft down sinking beneath her weight. The way he had held her, touched her, kissed her . . .

Sighing, she released a deep breath. There was no use dwelling on things she could not have. Cal was leaving. That was that. Any dreams of a large family with huge Christmas celebrations and big Sunday dinners were going to remain just that: dreams. One thing she knew for sure was that there was no other man for her than Cal McQue, faults and all.

Blowing out the lamplight, she listened to the water lap at the boat. A humid breeze floated in through the open window, ruffling her hair, rustling the sheets.

Jack stiffened at the sound of a sniffle, then sighed. Charley was crying again. Every night since she arrived, she'd cried quietly into her pillow. Jack tried to leave her alone, not wanting to intrude, but enough was enough.

"Charley?"

Jack propped herself up on her elbows. "Charley, I know you're awake." She lit the lamp. Soft orange shadows danced against the wall. "You might as well come out from under those covers and talk to me. I'm not going to let you be. Not this time."

Slowly, the white sheet covering Charley's head inched back. Red rings edged Charley's green eyes. "Sorry."

Drawing in a deep breath, Jack ached for whatever it was causing Charley pain. "For what?"

"For being such a nuisance." She sniffled. "I wish Cal had never brought me here. I'm nothing but trouble."

Cool wood floorboards creaked under Jack's bare feet as she crossed the small expanse to Charley's bed and sat on the edge. "What is it? For weeks now you've been upset."

Charley sat up, pushed the long golden hair back behind her ears. Her lower lip trembled. Moisture clung to her lashes, shimmering in the pale light. "Have you ever been in love, Jack? Really in love?"

Cal's image immediately burst forth in her mind, but she brushed it aside. She thought she loved him, but wasn't the least bit certain, never having been in love before. Surely she was no expert on the matter. Not confident as to what to say, she opted for honesty. "I don't know. Is that what all this crying is about? Love?"

Pressing her lips together, Charley nodded. "Why does it hurt so much?"

The deep chasm in Jack's chest echoed the sentiment. Was love supposed to hurt? Wasn't it supposed to be glorious? Sunshine and rainbows, not fire and brimstone?

"I wish I knew the answer to that, but I don't. Do you want to talk about it?"

Drawing her knees up under her chin, Charley wrapped her arms around her legs. She shrugged. "I'm in love. I have been for years now," she added, matter-of-factly.

Shocked, Jack fought to hide it. Charley was Lou's age, just over twenty. "Does Cal know?"

Charley lurched forward, grabbing Jack by the arms, her eyes wide, the color draining from her face. "No! You can't tell him. Promise me, Jack, that you won't tell him."

Jack covered Charley's hands with her own. She didn't know what to say, what to do. She was illadept at handling this sort of situation. Alex would be infinitely better at this than she. Taking hold of Charley's hands, she held them tight. "I won't tell."

Relief flooded Charley's face as she slumped back against the carved headboard. "Oh what a mess my life is."

Jack knew the feeling. A part of her wanted to share her own problems, open up to someone who would hold all the answers, but she knew the only person who could help her was her. Or maybe Cal. But going to him was out of the question. One look into her eyes would reveal all her feelings for him, and that was the last thing with which she wanted to burden him.

Instead of dwelling on her own problems, she decided to focus on Charley's. Maybe she could help somehow.

"If you don't mind me asking, how come you don't want Cal to know?"

"He wouldn't approve."

"Are you so sure?"

She nodded.

Sighing, Jack wondered if this man of Charley's had anything to do with Cal's gambling—and cheating. She'd already surmised that Charley was at the root of Cal's underhandedness, and that Charley knew nothing about it. Charley did not harbor the type of personality to keep such things quiet.

"Why do you think he wouldn't approve?"

Charley sighed. Pulling her long hair forward over her shoulder, she threaded her fingers through the golden locks. "Let's just say that my father cast a long shadow. A shadow that still covers the choices we, Cal and I, make in our lives."

Though Jack knew nothing about Cal's father, she could understand what Charley was saying. Hadn't her own father cast a long shadow? Not only in the way he brought up his children, but also in the honest and forthright way he ruled as a judge. It was a hard example to follow.

What had Cal's father been like? Thoughts and questions swirled in her head about the man who had raised Cal. Cal was such an odd mix of man. Honorable yet willing to cheat. Compassionate yet standoffish. Adventurous, loyal, mulish, spontaneous, hypocritical. Had his father possessed the same unusual combination of qualities?

"It's just such a mess, Jack. And I'm not sure what to do about it."

"Why doesn't this man of yours come talk to Cal, plead his case?"

Charley's eyes rounded in horror. "That would be an enormous mistake."

"Why?"

"It just would." Her chin inched up. "I need to figure out some way we can be together. I certainly don't
want to wait until I'm five and twenty to marry, as
Cal would have me do. It's been too long as is. I need
to find a way to be with the man I love without Cal
learning of it first. Once I marry, he'll have to accept
my husband."

Jack wasn't so sure. "Charley, Cal would be hurt
by your deception. Would you risk losing your
brother, your only family, for this man?"

Charley didn't answer.

Rising, Jack walked to the window and stared out
at the river, hoping to find some answers in its silvery
depths.

Slowly, she turned back to the bed. "Listen, Charley, Lord knows I'm the last one to preach about love,
but I agree that love is something special, truly a gift.
Certainly something worth taking risks for. However,
I think you're underestimating your brother. He's an
amazing man. He'll understand. Explain it to him."

Charley shook her head. "No, I can't. I have to do
it on my own."

Such stubbornness! No doubt she had learned the
trait from her hardheaded brother.

"He loves you, Charley." Jack folded her arms
across her chest. "And wants what's best for you."

Sliding back under the thin sheet on her bed, Charley said, "I know he does, Jack. But it's not his love
for me I'm worried about. He'll do anything in his
power to protect me. Even if I don't want his protection. And I don't particularly want to see my brother
murder the man I love because Cal doesn't deem him
worthy of my heart."

Jack stared. Charley was completely serious. "Who is this man?"

A dreamy smile crossed her lips. "His name is Daley Lombard."

Chapter Nine

The early morning sun filtered through the hazy clouds. Jack lifted her face to the warming rays.

A yawn escaped. She and Charley had spoken deep into the early morning about this mystery man of hers. From the sound of it, Mr. Lombard seemed to be a nice man. There was no telling why Charley thought Cal would harbor murderous thoughts toward him.

Did Cal already know him? Was there bad blood between them?

All were questions she would not likely ever have answers to. Because the only person who could answer them was Cal. And he was leaving.

Her stomach twisted painfully, as it always did when she considered the possibility of never seeing him again. Oh, how she already missed him. For nearly two weeks now she'd been evading him, testing herself as well as keeping her word to him to stay away. Would she always feel as she did now? As though she'd been thoroughly trampled by a team of wild horses?

It hurt to breathe, her chest was so tight. Just the

thought of never having Cal touch her, hold her, kiss her again, made her want to weep.

She steeled herself against the emotion. Staying away from him was supposed to help her prepare for his leaving, give her time to adjust. But instead, she'd felt nothing but pain for days. Damnable tears lurked too close to the surface. Nothing but the thought of being in Cal's arms offered her any comfort.

The river's steady ripples shimmered as they washed ashore. Jack watched hired hands as they hustled on and off the *Amazing Grace,* preparing for tonight's ball. Alex had somehow managed to pull the event together in no time at all. The ballroom looked sensational. So far all but a handful of tickets had been sold. After the *Enquirer* ran a piece about the ball in the society pages, word had spread. It was going to be the success Alex needed it to be, and Jack couldn't be happier for her.

If only she could be just as happy for herself.

She shuffled down the deck, watching the city come alive as the sun inched higher into the milky sky.

Her deadline was tomorrow. What on earth was she to do?

Charley's voice rang in her ears. *I have to do it on my own.*

She had been speaking of her unsteady relationship with Mr. Lombard, but Jack heard her own voice in Charley's words. How often had she said she needed to do things on her own, to test the bounds of her own independence? Too many times to remember. Why after all this time did her steadfastness rub the wrong way, like a shirt too stiffly starched?

It unnerved her to think that her stubbornness might not be a favorable trait. Had she been walking about with blinders covering the fact that people had tried to help her over the years, not just hinder her? Had she simply looked the other way in favor of staying true to the mulish behavior she'd become accustomed to?

It rankled.

How much, though? Enough to change? Enough to seek help now that she needed it more than ever? She thought so. She could at least try.

"You look very thoughtful this morning."

Jack smiled at her brother-in-law. "Just wool-gathering."

Matt leaned on the railing. A sunbeam highlighted his profile, causing his strong jaw to look even more pronounced. "Anything serious?"

"Hopefully not."

"Hopefully? Anything I can help with?"

Here was her chance. Words stuck in her throat. Who knew asking for help would be so hard? "Actually, if you have a minute, I need to speak with you. And Alex."

"Alex is with Lou."

"Even better."

Matt held open the door for her. "They're preparing appetizers." He laughed. "Don't look so appalled. It's under the watchful eye of Doc."

"Thank heavens."

Nerves rattled her every step as they went down the stairs leading to the galley. Her hands turned clammy.

"Is this about Cal?" Matt asked.

She stopped mid-stride and shook her head. "No."

"I thought it might be, is all."

"He's leaving."

Matt's large hand settled on her back, comforting her. "I know."

She nodded. "I thought you might. But do you know why?"

Matt drew in a deep breath. "I asked and he evaded. Something's not quite right."

"Do you think he's in trouble?"

They reached the landing. His gray eyes darkened. "Up to his ears, Jack. Up to his ears."

Alex and Lou looked up as they entered the galley. Lou's pale hair fell into her eyes. "Come to help?" she asked.

Jack took in the mess of fruits and vegetables piled high on the countertop. Surely, they could not poison anyone with carrots and strawberries, could they?

"Jack," Alex asked, her dark eyes wide. "Is something wrong?"

Jack's hands ached from being clenched so tightly. Matt nudged her forward.

"Can we sit?" she asked, motioning to a small table set against the wall. Her knees had gone weak.

It wasn't in her to ask for help of any sort. Her father had done his job well. She'd become fiercely independent over the years. If she had any other choice—any choice at all—she wouldn't be in this position.

Knowing this irritated her further. Making a conscious decision to ask for help hadn't been easy, but maintaining the vow she'd made to herself to become more open to help was going to be next to impossible.

Alex wiped her hands on a dishcloth. Her gaze skittered between Matt and Jack, her eyes wide, confusion etching fine lines into the corners of her mouth.

Lou's pale brows dipped as she too wiped her hands clean. Doc excused himself as Matt pulled out chairs.

Jack sat, her legs twitching. Something inside, down deep, tightened in the depths of her stomach as her family filled in around her. Surrounded her. As they always had.

It had never occurred to her before now that along with all the many uncommon lessons her parents had taught the three of them, there had always been other underlying messages: unity, loyalty, love.

She'd do anything for her sisters. And she suddenly understood that they'd do anything for her too. This realization loosened the knots in her stomach, took some of the tightness from her shoulders. She looked from face to face, saw the concern.

Lou placed her hand atop Jack's. "What is it?"

Jack drew in a long, calming breath. "It took seeing Cal and Charley for me to realize how selfish I've been."

"Selfish?" Alex's eyes narrowed. "Nonsense. There's not a selfish bone in your body."

Jack smiled inwardly. Alex, the protector. "I have been."

Lou squeezed Jack's hand. Her violet eyes glowed. "How so?"

"Charley refuses to share her worries with Cal. Cal refuses to share his troubles with Charley."

"With anyone," Matt added.

"Exactly," she said.

Alex's eyebrows dipped, but she remained silent. Jack pressed on before Alex could begin her interrogation.

"I see, as an outsider, that if they simply spoke to each other about their woes, they could help one another instead of carrying the burden alone."

Doc's whistling from the back room carried in the silence.

"I've seen," Jack said slowly, "that I've been selfish in not sharing my problems with all of you."

"Problems?" Storm clouds crossed into Lou's eyes.

Jack's leg tapped a furious beat. It was now or

never. "I need to borrow some money," she announced, then waited for their reactions. None came.

"How much?" Alex asked without hesitation.

"About a thousand dollars."

Lou's mouth opened into a small 'o'. Matt leaned back in his chair and looked at her, speculation bright and clear in his gaze.

Jack's stomach clenched as she added, "By tomorrow."

Lou's 'o' widened.

Alex placed her hand on Jack's. "I'll have it to you by the end of the day."

"I'll help also." Lou looked so determined Jack almost laughed, but she couldn't. Not with her throat's sudden tightness.

"Just like that?" she whispered. "No questions as to why I need it?"

Alex slipped her hand into Matt's. "It must be important for you to have asked. That's all that matters."

Lou smiled. "But if you're willing to share . . ."

Lord above, she loved her sisters. Which made it all the harder to say what needed to be said. "I'm going to buy some land."

Smugly, Matt grinned. To his wife, he said, "I told you so."

Jack's jaw dropped. "You knew?"

Lou's chair scraped across the wooden floor. She rose to give Jack a hug. "We all knew it was a matter of time."

Alex's eyes shone, but her smile grew. "We were wondering how long you'd feel obligated to stay on board, how long you'd deny your true desires."

"Is it nearby?" Lou asked. "We also had wagers on how far away you'd move. We know how much you love the West, Montana in particular."

"I do love the West, but I could never go alone. Even I'm not that brave."

"Nonsense," Matt murmured.

Alex swiped at her eyes. "I'm just so happy for you, Jack. Tell us everything."

Jack sat back in her chair and talked until she was nearly breathless. Odd, considering she was breathing easily for the first time in months.

If only she could get Cal to open up to her. Maybe then all her dreams would come true.

Chapter Ten

Jack stood outside the ballroom door. The joyful cries of a violin carried out to her on the deck, but she wasn't quite ready to join the festivities.

It was only because of Alex's unsubtle hints that she was here at all. Attending this infernal ball was the least she could do to repay her sisters' kindness. As promised, Alex had delivered a thick band of money to her earlier in the day. Tomorrow she would take it to Mr. Searcy and the land would be hers.

All her own.

Jack couldn't help the smile that formed as she fastened a bandit's mask tightly around her head, fluffing the red kerchief around her neck. Absently, as she paced the deck, she noticed a bounce in her step that had been missing for quite a while. It had returned, thanks to her sisters. Oh, how she loved them. And Matt and John too.

It struck her as funny just how far they had come. A mere six months ago, they had been arguing about who was to marry first. A battle Alex had lost. Thankfully. If Alex's marriage to Matt hadn't financially provided for Jack and Lou as well, they would have had to marry for convenience. Which sounded about as appealing as eating something one of her sisters had cooked.

It seemed fate had smiled on them, bringing love into their lives. For Alex and Lou, the love they found with their husbands was nothing less than magnificent. The love—if that's what it was—she'd found with Cal, however, seemed to be headed to a bittersweet end.

A couple brushed past her, dressed as George and Martha Washington. Jack stepped aside, considering her own costume as she did so. It wasn't much but it was a sight better than the costume Alex had chosen.

Though she felt as though she owed her sisters, the bounds of her debt went only so far. There was no way on God's green earth that she was going to wear the monstrocity Alex had handed her earlier that afternoon.

Josephine, Alex had said, a bright smile lighting her brown eyes.

To Jack it simply looked painful. With stays and ties and corsets and petticoats. It baffled her to no end as to why Alex had chosen the outfit at all.

Instead, Jack had thrown together a costume of her own—one that truly represented who she was. It didn't take much imagination to choose the black pants, fringed black shirt, dark boots and a jet-black hat. All items she already possessed. A red kerchief tied around her neck had added a splash of color that complemented her skin tone amazingly. Not that she held such matters with any regard. At least, she admitted, when she knew Cal was not going to be around.

Deciding she'd procrastinated long enough, she

stepped into the ballroom. Her mouth dropped open slightly as she took it all in.

Alex had created a lovely wonderland of bright colors, soothing scents, wonderful sounds, and breathtaking beauty.

Her gaze swept over the fabric-draped walls, the flowing, fluttering ribbons, the dimmed lighting that resembled twinkling stars.

In awe, she continued to look around, to absorb the magic. Couples glided along the polished floor, swaying in rhythm to the music.

Jack smiled, caught up in the moment.

"Someone might think you're having fun by looking at that smile. Are you?" Lou stood at Jack's elbow, looking elegant and lovely draped in swaths of sheer fabric, delicate gossamer wings trembling on her back.

A more beautiful pixie Jack had never seen.

"I think I am," Jack admitted reluctantly. Being here, amidst this lovely setting had brought on a peacefulness long lacking in her life.

"What happened to your costume?" Lou queried, pouring red punch into a glass cup.

Jack rocked on her heel. "This *is* my costume."

Sipping through smiling lips, Lou said, "I thought I heard Alex mention Josephine, not Jesse James."

Watching as dancers twirled, Jack thought, not for the first time, how grand it would be to float effortlessly through the air, linked to the man you loved.

"The bounds of my gratitude go only so far. Where's John?" she asked, as she spotted Alex and Matt drift by, their eyes locked on each other.

Lou motioned to the corner of the room. "He's been cornered by Mr. and Mrs. Mason."

"Are you singing tonight?"

Color rushed into Lou's cheeks. After months of

singing as Madame Angelique with no qualms at all, singing as Lou Hewitt still brought a blush to her sister's pale face. "One or two songs."

"Wonderful."

Lou watched her husband. "I suppose I should go rescue him."

Jack smiled as she saw John peering over the top of Mrs. Mason's ornate hat, looking like a man lost. "It would be the wifely thing to do."

"You'll be all right alone?"

Where was this coming from? She had been alone more often than not during her twenty-three years. "Just fine."

As she watched Lou float across the floor, she noticed several heads turn in Lou's wake. She was that lovely.

A slice of envy crept up as she saw Lou slide her arm across John's back, lean into him.

What was it like, she wondered, to be so free with your emotions? To touch whenever you wished? To kiss when the mood struck?

Unfortunately she would never know. Such affections were reserved for husbands and wives, sweethearts and beaus.

None of which she had, and with Cal leaving soon, would never have.

Sadness settled in, blocking her earlier euphoria at having gained enough money to finally buy her own land. Land that came at a high cost.

The cost of never seeing Cal again.

Trying to bolster her mood, she reminded herself that she had another week with him. A week, perhaps, with which she could convince him to stay.

A grumble in her stomach led her to a table piled high with all sorts of mouthwatering delights.

Tiny puffs filled with cream tempted her until she remembered Alex and Lou had been working in the kitchen that morning. The risk of poisoning was too great to take. She chose instead a skewer of strawberries, pineapple, and cantaloupe melon.

An unfamiliar male voice rumbled beside her. "Is there something I should know about the cream puffs?"

Jack turned to the man at her side. "Pardon?"

"You looked as though one of the tasty treats might sprout eight legs and crawl away. Is there something wrong with them? Or perhaps you simply hold an aversion to all things pastry?" His full dark mustache with curling ends quivered as he smiled.

His good humor had a contagious effect. Jack returned his smile. "Neither. I'm sure they're perfectly delicious."

Probably.

After all, with Doc overseeing Alex and Lou's efforts, how awful could they be?

"Said a woman who looks like she just bit into a sour grape."

His mischievous brown eyes sparkled. The wooden mask he wore was a carved relief of some sort, arcing above his eyes, sloping over his cheeks. His mustache, mouth, and strong chin were left uncovered.

She didn't particularly want to see him poisoned either. "Perhaps, er, you'd care for some fruit?"

He watched her, a speculative glint in his eye as he picked up a skewer of fruit. Silver strands liberally streaked his dark hair, but there were no lines creasing his lips, his eyes. She gauged him to be about Cal's age, or thereabouts.

"That's an unusual mask."

Gently, he touched it. "I made it myself."

Her eyes went wide. "How amazing. You're very talented."

Bowing slightly, he said, "I thank you. Though my true love is furniture making, I like to dabble in other areas as well."

She smiled. "You dabble well."

He plucked a pineapple chunk from the skewer, and asked, "Might you be Miss Jack Parker?"

A piece of strawberry lodged in her throat. She coughed rather indelicately. "Do I know you?"

"I don't believe so, but I've heard much about you."

Jack set her skewer down. There was no hope for eating tonight. Either she'd be poisoned or choke to death. "Dare I ask?"

He laughed. Truly, it was the most infectious sound. Twirling the end of his mustache, he said, "Let's see. 'Fabulous, independent, brave, headstrong, lovely, talented, loyal—' "

Jack held up her hand, stopping him. "Obviously you've been listening to someone who has mistaken me for another."

"Not so."

"Then clearly someone in need of a good physician."

He laughed, setting his skewer aside. His tone turned serious. "I think Charlotte would disagree."

"Charley?"

He stood about Cal's height, but thicker through the shoulders and waist. He leaned in. "She speaks quite highly of you."

Jack knew nothing of Charley having made a friend in Cincinnati. All she ever spoke of these days was . . .

Jack smiled, but noticed he looked over her shoulder, a very serious expression on his face. His brown eyes darted back to her. "I'm sorry, Miss Parker, but I must take leave of your delightful accompaniment."

"It was a pleasure meeting you, Mr. Lombard."

He grinned quite like a cat that had just eaten the pet canary. "Clever. Ah yes, I believe Charlotte mentioned that as well." His gaze lingered over her shoulder. "A pleasure."

He bowed and slowly retreated. "Perhaps we can continue this conversation another time?"

Curious, Jack peered over her right shoulder. Nothing was amiss. "I look forward to it," she said, turning back to him, only to find that he had disappeared.

"How peculiar," she murmured under her breath, plucking a grape from its stem.

An odd current in the air lifted her head, and caused her to look around.

As her gaze settled on the tall, costumed man fidgeting in the doorway, she smiled.

It was lucky she loved her sisters, otherwise she just might need to maim them for using their matchmaking tendencies on her. But at least she now understood the Josephine costume. She grabbed two glasses of punch and headed over to the doorway, toward Cal.

Cal walked into the ballroom, unable to believe he'd agreed to this farce.

The abysmal three-cornered hat teetered on his head, wobbling with each step he took. He'd give it another quarter hour, then he'd pitch the blasted thing into the river.

Candlelight danced from the chandeliers, scattering shadows throughout the lushly decorated room. A soft breeze blew in from the southern-facing windows, offering slight relief from the stuffiness.

Punch glasses chiming together provided delicate accompaniment to the eight-piece ensemble, currently playing a waltz.

He looked around for Charley. The sooner they danced, the sooner he could leave. His feelings of brotherly inadequacy only stretched so far. And with this room, and these people, and this appalling costume, he was near his breaking point.

Add the fact that Charley was nowhere to be found and his last nerve frayed.

"I always pictured you as a Blackbeard type. Napoleon seems so beneath you, Cal."

He froze. This night had officially turned tortuous. And that fraying nerve just snapped.

Slowly, he turned. "I thought you weren't coming."

Jack's skin glowed in the soft light. She'd left her long hair down and it swayed and shimmered across her back. Happiness danced in her eyes beneath a bandit's mask and under the shadows of her hat. "I didn't think I was either."

The words he'd spoken the last time they were together came rushing into his head. *Charley and I will be gone in two weeks' time, until then please just stay away from me. I do not want to start something with you that I know I cannot finish . . . So, please.*

Glancing up at him, there was something in her eye that dared him to remind her of what he'd said. He kept quiet, wishing he'd done so a week ago. He'd missed her.

She handed him a glass of punch. He hoped someone had taken mercy on him and emptied a flask of whiskey into the glass as well. He sipped, then frowned. It was to be a tortuous night through and through. "Flour bags were mentioned, I believe."

She laughed, her whole facing lighting up. It had

been some time since he'd seen her this way. So vibrant. So happy.

A dull pain began to pulse behind his eyes, distant yet persistent. Why was she so happy when he was so miserable? Unless . . . Unless she was happy he was leaving.

The pain intensified, small drumbeats echoing through his head. His gaze fell to her lips, lips he missed kissing, and he noticed that she was talking. He'd missed most of what she'd said.

". . . Alex happy."

"Hmmm?"

One of her dark eyebrows lifted. "I said it's nice to see Alex happy."

Alex and Matt were waltzing, their eyes solely on each other. Alex wore a billowy dress that enhanced her tall frame, and Matt . . . He couldn't quite tell whom Matt had dressed as. To Cal's eye he looked to be wearing a simple black suit and black mask.

It made Cal feel even more ridiculous with his ruffled shirt, tight coat, and short knickers.

"Cal?" Jack looked at him, questioning.

"Yes, she does look happy. Radiant." He couldn't help but watch Jack as he spoke the words. Her smiled faltered as she looked up at him and wet her lips.

His stomach tumbled.

Jack's shoulder bumped his. Her eyes flew open as she took a step away from him, apparently feeling the heat coursing between them that had nothing to do with the summer night.

Her look of joy vanished, replaced now with skittish apprehension. He took hold of her arm before she could flee.

"Dance with me."

Her mouth opened into a small 'o'. She shook her head.

"Please?"

The long smooth column of her throat rippled as she swallowed. "I don't know how."

"I'll teach you."

"I'll fall."

"I'll catch you."

Her blue eyes darkened.

"Don't you trust me?" he asked.

Chin high, she stared at him. His heart hammered. It seemed as though he was asking for much more than a dance.

Finally, she said, "I do."

He took her cup from her tight fingers and placed it on a sideboard next to his. Slowly, he lifted her hand, trailed a finger over her palm, and felt her shiver.

Pulling her closer to him than was appropriate, he could feel her heart pounding against his chest. His heart returned the beat, measure for measure.

She removed her hat. The weight of it rested on his back as she wrapped her arm around him. Her sleek black hair swung silky smooth over his hand.

The music faded as he concentrated on her, on holding her, on telling her with his eyes how he truly felt about her.

Other dancers blurred around them as her deep blue eyes kept him captive. There was no apprehension lingering in her gaze. Just trust, as he guided her across the floor.

The ache in his head diminished, nearly disappearing completely. He could see so much in her gaze. And all of it spoke of love and laughter, happiness and a future—the two of them together.

If only he didn't leave her. If only.

Which was impossible.

Charley's future depended on him. She had her whole life wide open before her. He needed to be there for her, to prevent her from making the same error in judgment as their mother had, from taking the responsibility of the Double C on herself.

It was his duty. A duty left to him by a father who'd failed them both. He would not flounder like his father had.

Jack stepped on his toe, and smiled when he grunted.

"You did that purposely," he accused.

"Perhaps. But then perhaps you should be paying attention to me instead of wool-gathering."

He gathered her close, loving the feel of her soft curves against the hard planes of his body. "Is that so?"

Her blue eyes had gone wide, and her mouth had parted slightly. She wet her lips as a slash of color swept onto her cheeks. "It is."

"Why?"

The nub of her chin shot out. "If I am to have you but for another week, I'd like to make the most of it, that is, if you want me."

He groaned. He wanted her more than anything.

One week.

His chest tightened painfully. His head pounded as it occurred to him that after this week was through he'd probably never hold her this tightly again. Never feel this whole again. Something had to be done.

Stiffening, he held her at arm's length. "Come outside with me."

She tipped her head. "Why?"

His hand tight on hers, he tugged her toward the door.

"Cal, what's wrong?"

He stopped short. "Do you trust me?"

"I said I did."

The fierceness of her tone made him smile. "Then come with me."

He just hoped she trusted him enough to follow him to Louisville. Just because he had to be there didn't mean he had to go alone.

Chapter Eleven

Beneath the diamond stars and bright moon, Jack could feel herself slipping into the magic of the night.

Out here on the deck, a soft breeze carried the music to them as she and Cal walked to the railing and stared downriver, a winding silver swath in the moonlit night.

Tempting the fates, she leaned into Cal, molding herself against his solid strength. His arm curled around her, pulling her closer. His cheek curved against her forehead and she felt the whisper of a kiss along her hairline.

She feared speaking would break the magical spell that had been cast tonight and she simply did not want to return to reality.

Not yet.

Even though she knew something was on Cal's mind. Something important. If he was content to let it be for the moment, then so was she.

Cal's soft, rhythmic breathing pulsed against her ear. Stirring to life those languorous feelings buried deep in her heart. Whatever was she to do without him?

A shiver trickled down her spine at the thought and Cal held her tighter still.

"You couldn't possibly be chilled."

Only by the thought of losing him. "Not with you by my side."

"Jack . . ."

She turned in his arms, pressing her face in the crook of his neck. Their two hearts beat against each other.

Breathing deep, she drew in that masculine mix of sunlight and musk, two common scents whose fusion was uniquely his own. Oh, how she'd miss it, miss him.

Tears stung and she blinked them back. Looking up at him, his green gaze bore into her, seeming to look deep inside, past her defenses and straight into her heart.

I love you. She let the words shine through her eyes. The truth of it was still too raw, too bare to share with him aloud. Yet she hoped he could hear it, deep in his soul.

Looking far into his eyes, she searched for a reciprocation of her feelings. And through the hazy mist of silver-green, she found what she had been seeking as he let down his guard, let her into his heart.

His hand cupped her cheek. "Oh, Jack."

As if she were dreaming, he slowly lowered his head and sought her lips with his own, sending her heart jumping about crazily in her chest.

His kiss sent her soaring. High above all rational reasoning, above all reminders that she should be protecting her heart, not giving it to him so completely. Giving it to him to break.

His warm hand settled on the back of her neck, his fingers tangling in her hair. Each tug carried delicious quivers down her spine.

With slight pressure, he deepened his kiss, and she not only lost all sense of time and place, but of self too.

Slowly, her hands inched upward, over the ruffles of his ridiculous shirt. A whisker-roughened chin scraped the pads of her fingers as she sought to trace every line, every plane.

Heat rushed into her face, her neck. To every nook and cranny her body possessed all the way down to her little toe. Along her back, his hand slipped down her spine, adding spirals of fire to her already simmering blood.

Much too soon, he pulled away. There were so many new feelings to explore, to examine. Unabashedly, she silently admitted she wanted more. More of precisely what remained unclear, but she longed for something she knew she could never have.

Her heart cried.

"You're so lovely." His rough voice washed over her as he pushed a strand of her hair behind her ear. "So very lovely."

Though her heart ached, she managed a smile. "You're not so bad yourself. Ruffles and all."

His wry grain nearly stole her breath. "The things I'm forced to do, all in the name of brotherly duty."

"You're a wonderful brother."

He let go of her, darkness creeping into his eyes, and she wondered at the troubles he kept to himself. The troubles that somehow involved Charley.

Not wanting to ruin their special moment, she didn't ask him about his worries. She sought to put him at ease, at least whcre she was concerned.

Taking a deep breath, she said, "I have some news, Cal. Good news."

* * *

"Good news?" Cal ran his hands down her arms. He couldn't seem to stop touching her. What would she say when he asked her to join him on the Double C? It was true, it wasn't what either of them wanted necessarily, but they would be together. And that's all that mattered.

A ball of nerves bounced around his stomach. Why couldn't he just voice the words? For the past ten minutes he'd struggled with what to say, how to say it.

He felt like an awkward adolescent. Why was it so hard to open his heart to her? Why, when his love for her was already deeply rooted within it?

Wind tousled her long, sleek hair. She pushed a hand through it, securing wayward strands behind her ears. "I'm turning over the running of the gaming hall to Matt." Her eyes bright and earnest, she said, "I'd planned on passing it to you, Cal, where I'd know it would be in good hands. The news that you're lea—" She cleared her throat. "*Leaving* hit me hard. Matt will do a fine job of it, though. Perhaps not as good as you, but—"

He cut in. "How is that good news? After all the effort you've put into it?" He let go of her, backing up to get a better look at her face.

Moonlight washed over her full cheeks as she looked up at him. Her dark blue eyes seemed black in the night, but the moon illuminated specks of color. Sparkling sapphires. "It's a good thing because I have another job to do."

Cold dread stroked his spine. In his head, he'd had their future all planned. She'd come with him to Louisville, help work the Double C, but return to the *Amazing Grace* when needed. However, a new job? That turned his plans inside out.

"What kind of job? In another gaming hall?"

A stab of jealousy took him by surprise. And he hated himself for it. He'd had years to open his own saloon, but he hadn't. He'd let his childhood push him into a life of wanderlust. A life, he daresay, that now filled him with unhappiness. And now that he had finally come to terms with exactly who he was, there was nothing he could do about it. Because like his childhood, his life seemed to be at the mercy of his father's misdeeds.

Jack slipped out of his arms and stared out at the river. He stepped up next to her, the sleeve of his Napoleon jacket brushing her arm.

She looked up at him. "No, not gambling. I've always loved to gamble, but solely for the thrill of it. And maybe because I wasn't supposed to do it." She flashed a smile. "You know how I feel about insensible rules. Gaming is not in my blood like it's in yours."

In his blood. Indeed. He had to remind himself that he was not like his father. His father had gambled as an addiction. His own passion came from the intricacies of the game. Until this mess with Charley, he set no store in winning. Or losing. It had been solely about playing.

Why, he wondered, had it taken him so long to realize gambling wasn't just a pastime for him, but his way of life? If he'd figured that out sooner, then maybe he'd have opened his own saloon by now, or a gambling club like the Maybury years ago.

But then he'd have never met Jack.

With the uncasy feeling that all he'd ever wanted was slipping through his fingers, he gripped the railing tightly. Nervousness strained his voice. "What're you going to do?"

She smiled up at him. Happiness shone off her, a beacon in the dark night. "I've bought a ranch."

Cal swallowed. Hard. He battled back a wave of self-pity. His life was as he'd made it. There was no one to blame but himself. He blamed himself for realizing, too late, what he wanted out of life. A life that included Jack in it and just wasn't possible.

"Have you now?"

Tipping her head to the side, she looked at him, a question in her eyes.

His foul mood certainly wasn't her doing, and he tried to put some cheer into his voice to mask the pain. "Tell me about it."

"It's twenty acres out near River Glen. Rolling meadows, ponds, stables. I'll have to start out slowly, pick a few quality horses. Soon enough I hope to have a whole stable full of superior horses that would equal, if not surpass, the farms in Lexington."

The exuberance in her voice took the edge off his misery. "Sounds wonderful. When are you leaving?"

"Not for a while." She laughed. "I've got to give Mr. Searcy the rest of the money for the land first."

He stiffened. "The rest of the money?"

Her eyes wide and wary, she said, "Yes. I gave Mr. Searcy money to hold the land for me with the agreement that I'd pay in full by the end of the month— tomorrow. I'll ride out early and collect the deed."

Perhaps because he'd been raised by a con artist, a multitude of concerns jumped into his thoughts. "This agreement is in writing, of course?"

Laughter floated out to them. Gentle strains of a lighthearted ballad carried. Neither soothed his tortured soul.

"Of course." She reached up, pressed her thumb between his eyebrows. "Now stop worrying, Cal. You're giving yourself wrinkles."

Before he could think not to, he captured her hand, brought it to his lips for a kiss. "I'm allowed to worry about you."

Moist lips parted. "Oh?"

"Absolutely."

"Then I am to worry about you also."

Pressing her hand to his cheek, he leaned into it. "It doesn't work both ways, Jack."

Her voice was but a whisper in the wind. "That's where you're wrong, Cal. It does work both ways."

Wrapping her free arm around his waist, she pushed close to him. "Will you tell me about Charley now?"

Hearing Charley's name sparked his memory. Holy heavens! Until now, he'd totally forgotten tonight's high stakes poker game. Being with Jack had pushed all thoughts of time away and, judging by the position of the moon, he was already late.

"I've got to go," he said, pulling away. If he won the pot tonight, he'd have more than enough to release Charley from the binds of that promissory note.

Jack blinked in confusion. "Where?"

Shaking his head, he said, "Out."

She set her hands on her hips and frowned at him, her lips pulling downward. "You won't tell me."

"No."

"Why not?"

"I don't have time to argue, Jack." He checked his pocket watch. Would they start the game without him? "You're going to have to trust me."

"You're not making it easy." She fluffed the ruffle on his shirt. "Trust goes both ways, Cal. If you want me to trust you then you have to share your trust with me."

The steamboat rocked as her words struck him hard. He'd never thought of it that way, but she was right. She did deserve the truth. "Meet me tomorrow morning. Right here. I'll explain everything."

"Promise?"

After pressing a kiss to her forehead, he inched backward, toward the doors. "Promise."

Turning on his heel, he barely heard Jack's parting words: "Be careful."

Chapter Twelve

Cal's mood was foul when he walked into O'Malley's, and four hours later, despite his mounting winnings, it had not improved.

Usually it was places like O'Malley's that put him at ease. There was a sense of home in these saloons, with the Irish music, the old friendships of the customers, and the lively games.

But tonight, the pain in his head raged. It took nearly all his concentration to play. To play fairly, he might add. His promise to Jack had hit hard. He didn't want to live a life he despised. He'd earn the money to repay Daley Lombard, and he'd win it without the dark cloud of cheating hanging over his head. He was not his father, never would be, and that was all there was to it.

After playing his last card, he decided it was high time to quit while he was ahead. He scooped his winnings—winnings that would more than erase the debt owed to Daley Lombard—and nodded to the men whose pockets he'd emptied.

The one closest to him leaned in to shake his hand. "Name's Larson. Good playing."

The man had rough, thick hands. Cal swallowed the false name he usually used. If he was to truly step out of his father's shadow, he needed to own and accept his surname. "McQue. Cal McQue."

From behind him, he heard a sharp whistle. He turned to find a ruddy-faced man giving him a disdainful look. "You be any relation to Hoyt McQue?"

It came as no surprise that his father's name was known up in these parts. For years, Hoyt McQue traveled, perfecting his methods of cheating, stealing, and conning. He was a legend in most parts. Steeling himself, Cal said, "He was my father."

The man tapped his pool stick against the worn, planked floor. "Is that so?"

Cal folded his arms. "It is. Do you have something to make of it?"

The man chuckled. "Me? No. But I'd be thinking that those there men might have a word or two for the son of the most notorious sharpie east of the Mississippi. 'Specially with stakes as high as they were."

Cal stepped up to the man, chest to chest, and looked down into his rheumy eyes. He spoke through clenched teeth. "You accusing me of something?"

With shaky legs, the man stepped back. "I s'pose not."

"Then I'll be on my way." He tipped his hat to the men at his table. "A pleasure."

Turning on his heel, he fought a wave of nausea. Pain gripped his head like nothing else he'd ever felt. He reached for the door handle, hoping the night air would soothe the fire behind his eyes.

He'd taken a mere two steps when he heard footsteps behind him. Before he could look over his shoulder, he felt a sharp knock on his head, accompanied by a loud crack. Pain exploded. Bright colors flashed behind his eyes. Blazing reds and brilliant whites, dazzling yellows and vivid oranges.

Then his world went black.

"Jack!"

The door slammed open, knocking against the wall. A picture hanging nearby fell to the floor with a sharp thud. Jack jumped straight up in bed, blinking away any remaining vestiges of sleep.

She was on her feet, grabbing her wrap before her eyesight had fully adjusted. Charley paced a small square of the floor, wringing her hands.

The look on Charley's face filled Jack's stomach with dread. "What is it?"

"I gave him until three. He's never stayed out this late before. What's become of him? Why isn't he back?"

Jack lit the lamp, forced herself to calm. "Who?"

"Cal."

Peering at the table clock, Jack frowned. It was half past three now. "He's not back?"

"No. I've been waiting up for him. I wanted to speak to him about Daley . . ."

Jack pulled on her shirt, then tucked it into the trousers she had just shimmied into. Anger mingled with worry, creating a whirlpool of fear low in her belly.

She kept panic at bay by sheer will. It had been only a matter of time before Cal's gambling got him into trouble.

"Sit," she told Charley, forcing her down onto the bed. "I'm going to check the hospital."

Charlotte jumped up. "The hospital? You don't think . . ."

Jack pushed her down again. "If he's not there, I will start at one end of town and search every pub and tavern till I reach the other side. I'll find him." And kill him with her bare hands for putting her through this misery.

If he wasn't already dead.

She swallowed hard. She'd know, wouldn't she? Even as she thought it, though, uneasiness swelled inside. Something was wrong.

Twisting her hair up, she leveled a gaze at Charley. "Tell no one where I've gone. If I'm not back by first light, tell Alex I'm running errands."

Charley nodded numbly. "You will find him, won't you?"

"Yes." If anyone could find him, she could. She knew all the places he'd be able to find games this time of night.

As she stepped off the Landing, headed toward the hospital, she cursed Cal six ways to Sunday and back. He better not have gotten himself killed.

What would she do without him?

Three hours later, her temper was running near to its boiling point. She'd been to the hospital, even the jail. She'd been to too many pubs to count. The Maybury had closed its doors at one, so she didn't think Cal was there. Just to be sure, she checked the alleyways near the gaming hall.

How often tonight had she held her breath as she walked into an alley, praying for Cal not to be there banged up, bruised and battered, even dead?

Fists clenched, she barreled into Shea's, a seedy tavern on the outskirts of the city. She'd long since abandoned any niceties. The slamming of the door usually garnered the attention she desired. "Anyone see a man here tonight?" She gave a brief but accurate description of Cal, including the fact that he might have caused a bit of trouble. She made sure not to use his name, because she wasn't sure which he'd been using tonight. One of these blasted days he was going to tell her why he used an assumed name in the first place.

That was, if she found him. Alive.

Pushing negative thoughts aside, she searched the room, sighed at the negative response. "Thanks," she said, reaching for the door handle.

"Hey." Someone grabbed her arm.

Her heart kicked against her breastbone. Fears about her being a woman out on the streets this time of day hadn't come close to her worries about Cal's safety. Until now. Had someone recognized her as a woman through the thick clothes, lowered hat, and phony deep voice?

She stiffened, but turned, vowing to show no fear. She looked up at the man. "Yes?"

"The man you're looking for. His name McQue?"

Her breath hitched. "Yes."

"Any good reason you'd be looking for that diddler?"

Oh no, oh no. A diddler was a common term for a cheat. The anger in her tone wasn't faked. "Diddler or no, he's my Pa," she said. "And Ma's fit to bust a gut, worried about him. Didn't come home."

The man let go of her arm, stepped back. "I heard tell he made a ruckus over at O'Malley's."

She knew where it was. "You know if he's still there?"

Grim lines creased his mouth. "If they haven't strung him up yet."

Jack tipped her hat. "Thanks much."

"I wouldn't be announcing you as McQue's kin, giving the way they're thinking over there."

Stowing away that piece of advice, Jack set out in

the dusky morning light. Her boots clicked irritably on the cobblestone. Fists clenched, she rushed toward O'Malley's. Anger pulsed through her blood, pulled at her heart.

Did he cheat tonight? He'd promised her he wouldn't. She pulled up short, took a deep breath. He'd promised her. And she loved him enough to believe he wouldn't break that promise, no matter what. She'd keep her faith until she heard his guilt from his own lips.

Light glowed dimly from behind O'Malley's windows. Taking a deep breath, she opened the door, then sidled up to the bar. There were only a few men gathered here at this hour, talking quietly around the rims of their glasses. Whether they were early risers or had been here all night, she hadn't a clue. She just hoped someone was willing to tell her what happened to Cal.

She ordered up a pint from a bleary-eyed keeper. "Long night?" she asked in the gravelly voice she was coming to despise.

"I've had longer."

She sipped at the foamy beer, trying not to wince as the strong liquid slid down her throat.

With the keeper not willing to talk, she ambled over to a table where she could eavesdrop on the men nearby. It didn't take long for her to hear about Cal's misadventures. And only a few minutes more before one of the men bragged about taking Cal down a notch.

"The son of Hoyt McQue, who'd have thought?" she heard one man say.

Hoyt McQue?

She set her mug down. She'd never connected the name before. With a father like the infamous Hoyt

McQue no wonder Cal used false names when he gambled.

One of the men laughed, jarring Jack out of her silent confusion. She had to find Cal. It was obvious he was hurt somewhere. And since these men looked as though they were cemented to their chairs, she was thinking Cal couldn't be all that far off.

A hazy sunrise filled the sky to the east. Vendors were out, setting up their stands for the start of the day. Soon people would be rising for morning services.

O'Malley's abutted shops on each of its sides, but farther down the road, the mouth of an alley lay dark in the shadows between two old brick storefronts.

Jack picked her way along the buildings, dread rising with each step she took.

Splinters of light pierced the dark alleyway, leading her further. Among boxes of trash and old debris, Jack searched.

"Cal?" she called out, her voice echoing.

A rat scurried over her boot, and she jumped back, her heart pounding. Her anger had long since been silenced, replaced now with an aching hope that Cal was fine, as delusional as that hope may be.

Chest tight, Jack lifted crates and shifted newspapers. She stepped over a mound of trash and stifled a scream as she spotted a boot in the muddy light.

She stared at the heap of man covered with newspaper for a long while before she found the courage to lift the papers from the form.

With jerking motions, she removed the paper one piece at a time, slowly revealing Cal's prone, still body. He lay on his side and it was impossible to tell whether his chest rose and fell.

Heart in her throat, the echo of blood pounding her

ears, she lifted the last sheet from Cal's face. At the sight of it, she dropped to her knees next to him. Tears broke free of their dam and coursed down her cheeks.

He was alive.

"Cal?"

A large bruise circled his right eye, and a small cut near his lip looked sore as all get out. She ran a hand over his silky hair, feeling a goose egg near the crown of his head. Gently, she pressed. He moaned.

"Cal," she said a bit louder.

She wondered what wounds lay beneath his clothes, under his skin. Broken ribs, bruises? She knew of men who had died from a beating due to bleeding on the inside, and she prayed that Cal wasn't going to be one of them.

Pressing her cheek close to his, she couldn't help but brush his lips with a soft kiss. Her tears fell onto his face, running down his chin, slipping onto his neck. "Cal," she whispered, knowing she should go for help, but not wanting to leave him.

"You're getting me wet."

Jack jumped back, her hand over her mouth as she stared at his mischievous green gaze. She couldn't help the sobs that escaped just knowing that he could make light of his situation. He'd be okay. Relief coursed through her, washing out any doubts about his condition.

His hand snaked out to touch her knee. She clasped it, not knowing what to say, where to start. So for a long while, she said nothing at all. Just sat with him in the fetid darkness of the alley.

She swiped the tears from her eyes. "Let's get you home," she finally said. "Can you walk?"

As he rose to a sitting position, he went green in the face. Great gulps of air seemed to help, because a moment later, his color had returned, albeit a bit paler than his normal shade.

"Where do you hurt?" she asked.

"My head, my chest."

"Ribs?"

He nodded.

She locked her arms around his elbows, helping to lever him to his feet. All remnants of color drained from his face. She slipped her arm around him, felt his heart hammering against her ribcage.

"Jack, I didn't ch—"

"Didn't say you did."

"Just wanted you to know."

She smiled. "Now I do." It was nice to know her faith was justified.

Gently, she led him out of the alley, toward the light of daybreak. "We'll go slowly," she said.

Dawn spilled on them as they emerged from the alley. Out here, she could see how much pain he was in. Lips clenched in a tight grimace, he winced with every step. She felt his trembling as they stepped off the curbstone to cross the street.

Hiring a hack was not an option since it was so early on a Sunday morning. They'd have to make it back to the boat one torturous step at a time.

"Jack?"

She looked up at him, hoping he couldn't see her lingering worry. "Hmm?"

"Thank you."

She nudged him along. Biting back a line about him owing her, she said, "You're welcome."

Chapter Thirteen

Alex stood outside Jack's door, ear pressed firmly to the fine wood grain, listening for anything. Anything at all.

"Still nothing?" Lou asked in a soft whisper.

Alex shook her head.

"Think they're still in there?"

Jack and Cal had been in there all day. Alone. They'd sneaked on board sometime around dawn and neither hide nor hair of either of them had been seen since. It was now heading toward midnight, the dark sky filled with stars and the promise of a beautiful morning.

Lou's violet eyes shone. "Do you think . . ."

Alex didn't know what to think, quite honestly. Although she knew of Jack's feelings for Cal, she didn't think her sister would go so far as to . . . She swallowed. "I don't know."

A part of her wished Jack and Cal were doing exactly as she feared. Then the two could be forced to marry and put their hearts to peace at long last. Unfortunately, by the lack of sound emitting from the room, Alex had serious doubts anything of a carnal nature was taking place.

Lou seemed to be thinking along the same lines. "If Jack had a reputation to tarnish, this could look compromising."

A small thought wiggled into Alex's conscious. Jack's reputation, indeed. Ideas swirled. Yes, it was true the three of them had no reputation to speak of other than as odd misfits, but if there was a time to call importance to the damage done to a name from a night spent alone with a man, it was now.

Alex turned to Lou. A smile pulled at her lips. "Do you remember," she whispered, "when you and Jack blackmailed me into marrying Matthew?"

Confusion creased Lou's forehead. "Yes. I haven't gone daft."

Rolling her eyes, Alex pressed on. "I do believe it's time to return the favor."

Covering her gasp with her hand, Lou spoke through her fingers. "You don't mean . . ."

"It's quite obvious the two are meant for each other. Yet within days Jack will be off to her ranch alone, Cal off to Louisville. This may be our only chance."

Lou nodded. "It is for her own good. Though I daresay she's going to be a mite bit angry."

"As angry as I was when you and Jack first approached me?"

Lou smiled. "Point taken."

The baby kicked, and Alex instinctively placed her hand on her stomach to soothe the little one inside. "Let's wait until first light. More incriminating that way. And it will give us time to get everything ready before we knock. I'll gather up some flowers, a veil of some sort, and find Charley."

"I'll find the men, fill them in, and make sure John has his Bible with him."

Alex laid her hand on Lou's arm. "Remember, no matter how much she argues, we must stand firm on this."

Resolutely, Lou nodded. "Come tomorrow, our sister will be a married woman."

Alex smiled. "Whether she likes it or not."

Through heavy eyes, Jack watched Cal sleep. With some surprise, she realized he'd barely woken since collapsing into bed in the early hours. For most of the day she'd been torn between running for the doctor and inflicting more damage.

The few times Cal had woken, he'd begged off the doctor, saying all he needed was a little sleep. Sleep was perhaps what saved him from her wrath.

All curled into a little ball, he looked so vulnerable. Thoughts of pulling each hair from his head one by one had gone by the wayside with each ragged breath he took.

She tugged the blanket up to his chin. As they had all day, tears sprang to her eyes. He could have so easily been killed.

The lamplight flickered. Jack stared at the paneled walls, wondering when he would wake for a long period of time. Only then would she have the heart to leave him.

Perhaps she should have taken Charley up on her offer to sit with him, but at the time Jack hadn't wanted to leave his side.

Charley had been waiting for them on the stage when they hobbled up. Her horror-stricken face had done nothing to improve Cal's demeanor. It was best if Charley stayed away. At least for now. And with

Daley Lombard in town, Jack knew Charley would have something to keep her mind occupied.

Cal moaned as he tried to roll from his back to his side, his eyelids fluttering but not opening.

Legs aching, Jack stood, then checked on him for the hundredth time. Seeing that he still in fact breathed, she took a turn around his room, hoping to alleviate the soreness in her legs.

Stars twinkled in the dark night as she peered out the window. She checked the clock, wincing at the time. Somewhere around mid-afternoon, she had remembered her meeting with Mr. Searcy. Worry about losing the land had grown until she had forcefully banished the thoughts. There was nothing she could do about it now. Surely he'd give her a day reprieve. She'd make him understand. There was no way she was losing that land. It was all she had.

Almost all, she thought, sparing a look at Cal.

Her heart belonged to him almost as much as it belonged to her. There was no denying that fact. Wherever he went, it would go also. Whether he knew it or not.

She ran her hand over the dark planked walls as she walked about the room, lifting this, touching that. Near the door hung Cal's blood stained suit coat. It smelled horrible and would best be pitched into the boiler or buried.

Busying herself, she checked his pockets before ridding the room of the garment. His outer pockets held nothing, not even a stray piece of lint.

She supposed the men who attacked Cal had probably taken all his money. It seemed the likely scenario if they believed him cheating.

Her stomach swirled in a sea of doubt. He'd told her that he hadn't cheated again. She believed him.

However, something had possessed him to cheat once, some powerful motive he refused to share.

Frustration welled as she checked the inner pockets of the coat. Their conversation from last night came back to her, haunting her.

"Trust goes both ways, Cal. If you want me to trust you then you have to share your trust with me."

"Meet me tomorrow morning. Right here. I'll explain everything."

"Promise?"

"Promise."

Her hand dove into the last pocket in the coat and her fingers brushed against paper. Slowly, she pulled out a folded, worn piece of stationary and gasped as she opened it.

The stationary bore the name of Hoyt McQue. Cal's father.

She looked to the bed, to Cal's motionless form. Her morals waged war with her curiosity. After a long inner battle, she read the fine hand script, her horror growing with each passing word.

Legs shaky, she backed into the bedside chair, trying to absorb what she'd read. Her hand trembled as she reread the note—the promissory note. How could a father wager his daughter? It turned her stomach to think of the worry Cal must be going through.

But even more horrifying was the notion that Charley knew nothing of this, she couldn't. But more than that, did Mr. Lombard know of the note that bore the name of his father? she wondered.

Questions raged in her head. Too many to give thought to. Questions only Cal could answer.

She looked to the bed. He snored softly. Bruising colored the skin around his eye, the corner of his mouth. Yet, it did little to detract from his handsomeness. Oddly enough, the slight imperfections added to it. Letting that thought simmer, she realized she must be losing her senses from lack of sleep to think such a thing.

After rereading the letter once again, she sighed. Any questions she had would have to wait until Cal woke. He needed his rest and the last thing she wanted to do was disturb him.

She slipped the letter into her pocket, leaned back in the chair, and watched him sleep. As the hours drifted by, all she thought about was how close she'd come to losing him. And she knew, without a doubt, that she couldn't let it happen again.

She loved him.

So much so that she was willing to lay her heart on the line, bare all she felt for him, and let him make the decision.

The ranch, the land, meant nothing to her without him by her side. Without his touches and caresses. Without his tender whispered words.

She would tell him when he woke. If she didn't, she'd live a life of regret, of never knowing how he truly felt about her too. She would tell him, and maybe their honesty would lead to a future of love and happiness.

Her eyelids grew heavy, and she fought sleep as long as she could. In the end, it was a battle she lost.

Tingles of pain stabbed her foot. Sleepily, she shifted, rubbing at gritty eyes.

She looked to the bed, found Cal's green gaze studying her. "I think it's fair to say," he murmured in a roughened voice, "that you look worse than I do."

Immediately, she came fully awake. "How long have you been up?"

"Awhile. I didn't want to wake you." He tapped the magazine that was folded on his lap. "Interesting reading you have here." His dark eyebrows arched. "Care to tell me why you're still circling land in Montana if you've bought land here?"

She shrugged, poured water into a cup, and held it to his lips. His breath brushed her knuckles, sending a spiral of warmth down through her chest.

"Thank you," he murmured.

"You're welcome." She sat back down, her legs a bit weak.

"You didn't answer my question, Jack, about the land."

A loose thread on the chair called her attention. She picked and pulled at it. "Just silliness."

He reached over, stilled her hand. "I can see it's not."

She took his hand in hers, ran her finger over his knuckles. "Really, it is. Nothing could ever come of it."

Hair matted to his head on one side. She leaned over, ran her fingers through it, caressing its smooth silky waves.

"Why not?"

"Because I could never go it alone. Now could we please talk about something else?"

"Like?"

"Like you."

"What about me?"

She smiled at his teasing tone. "How do you feel?"

Cal struggled into a sitting position, his breaths harsh. "I'm right as rain."

Crossing her arms over her chest, she frowned. "So I see."

He winked. "You're a good nurse."

"You scared me."

"I know. I'm sorry."

"Please don't do it again."

He captured her hand, then kissed it. "I promise."

The words reminded her of another promise he'd made. But before she could ask about the note she'd found, he said, "Is all the money gone? My gun?"

"Everything but this," she said, pulling the note from her pocket. "I'm sorry."

His head dropped back against the pillow, his expression pained. "I was going to tell you today."

Her heart soared. He had been going to open up to her. That meant he cared, didn't it? "Yesterday," she automatically corrected.

Dark green eyes widened. "What day is it?"

Her gaze went to the window, at the colored fingers of first light. "Monday. Dawn, it looks like."

"You've taken care of me all that time?"

He made it sound as though she'd done something amazing. "You were asleep for most of it. I slipped out now and then when no one was standing guard outside to get a bite to eat. Are you hungry? You haven't eaten . . ."

He shook his head. After a moment, he motioned toward the note in her hand. "So you know."

Tipping her head to the side, she said, "I know what I read."

A scowl darkened Cal's bruised features. "He bartered his daughter."

She made no comment. It seemed to her that Cal had been speaking aloud to himself, more than looking for her to respond.

"What I don't know," she said, "is what you have to do with this. I assume this was the reason for your increased gambling?"

She left off any mention of his cheating. If it had been one of her sisters attached to that note, she'd have done anything—cheating included—to earn the money to repay the debt.

Memories of how desperate they'd been after their father died surfaced. If Matt hadn't taken on the *Amazing Grace,* who knows what lengths she'd have gone to to help provide for her family.

Yet, it still hurt just a bit to know Cal couldn't open up to her and share his worries, but she had forgiven his cheating the second she read the letter.

Eyebrows furrowed, he said, "There was a provision attached to that godforsaken thing that required the debt be passed on to me should my father die."

Horror rendered her speechless.

"I don't think my father meant to die before the debt was repaid, but be that as it may, he did." With a slightly shaky hand, Cal lifted the cup of water, took a long drink. "My father . . . he wasn't a bad man. I truly believed he loved us, but his gambling was like a sickness with him. He couldn't stop despite the ways it affected our family."

Jack rose, needing to be closer to him. The down mattress sank under her weight as she perched on the edge of the bed.

The lamp she'd lit last night glowed a soft orange, its flickering flame sending fragments of light dancing across the wall behind the bed.

She took Cal's hand and held it tight. She'd never seen him this way—so open and vulnerable.

"When I was ten, my mother passed away, tired and broken. She'd been a debutante when she married my drifter father—love at first sight. They'd moved to the ranch, land my mother's family had owned, and tried to make a life for themselves. But he couldn't control his urges, no matter how much he loved my mother. He was devastated by her death, just torn apart."

Tracing tiny circles in the palm of his hand, Jack tried her best to offer comfort. She had the uneasy feeling Cal had never spoken of this to anyone. Her heart nearly burst with the trust he was placing in her.

More than ever, she wanted to tell him she loved him. That she had loved him since the day she found him in the bathtub back in River Glen, but her declarations could wait, wait until he shared his life with her.

"He took to the road, making a name for himself by conning and cheating." He shook his head. "I was left to raise Charlotte along with our ranch foreman, Grogan. Looking back, I can see he raised us both."

"He did a fine job," she said, trying to soothe.

"Did he?" Cal asked sharply.

She captured his gaze, held it, letting her love shine through. "I think so, yes."

Sounding tired and weary, he sighed. "I'm a cheat, Jack. Just like my father."

Anger welled. "Only because of this." The promissory note crumpled beneath her fingers.

"It doesn't matter why. Just that I am." He gripped her hands, squeezed. "I can never be my own man. Not with my name. The other night proves that. Once those men learned who my father was, everything changed and look at the result."

She took in his bruised, swelled eye, the cracked lip. "You *can* be the man you want to be."

"I can never open a gaming hall of my own without my character being constantly cast in doubt. Not around these parts."

She conceded that he might be right. "That may be so."

"Not that it matters. My place is on the Double C with Charlotte."

Then that was where her place was too. "How are we going to deal with this note?" she asked. "I assume the money lost the other night was to repay this debt." She loved him, and in her mind neither of them would have to be alone.

"We?" he asked.

The corner of her mouth twitched. "We," she said firmly, brooking no arguments. The time was right to tell him of her feelings, to voice the love she had for him. To tell him that a future without him just wasn't worth the trouble. Softly, she said, "Cal, I—"

He interrupted, obviously not having heard her. "Without that money, there's only one thing left to do."

She swallowed hard. There was time enough to tell him that she loved him. "What's that?"

"Kill Daley Lombard."

Jack gasped. Shock rippled up and down her spine. "Daley Lombard?" Charley's beau couldn't know about this note. He was too much a gentleman to be a part of something so . . . so vile.

Cal exhaled. "George Lombard passed on a year back. I thought this note would be null and void, but the younger Lombard came to me two months back saying he was calling the debt due. We had been close once as children, but once our fathers turned against one another, our friendship died. I mourned it for a while, but him coming to me with this note proves he turned out just like his conniving father."

Jack swallowed hard. "Why? Why enforce the note?" she asked, not sure she wanted to hear the answer.

"We have adjoining land. For years the Lombards

wanted the land, but since it had belonged to my mother, my father couldn't wager it. Thankfully, or I suspect it would be long lost in a card game."

"Didn't your father inherit it?"

Cal's lips turned upward in a grim smile. "No. My mother left it to Charlotte. The only way to gain that land is through her."

"By marriage."

"Exactly. Because she loves that land too much to ever sell it."

Jack felt sick. Charlotte fancied Daley Lombard in love with her when he was simply using her . . .

Now she understood Mr. Lombard's unease at the ball. If Cal had recognized him . . . How could she have been so fooled by his charm? Usually she had such a keen eye to character.

A sickening notion came to mind. Charley had been alone with Daley Lombard all day. What if he was determined to get Charley's land at any cost? Even by manipulating a young innocent.

"What?"

"Daley Lombard . . . He's—"

A loud knock made her jump. Her heart lodged in her throat.

"Cal? Jack?" Vigorous knocking shook the door on its hinges. "Open up. It's Matt."

"And Alex."

"And Lou."

"And Charley."

Jack let out a breath of relief. If Charley was with Alex and Lou she must be fine. Even still, she needed to alert Cal to Mr. Lombard's presence.

Her relief vanished in a flash the instant another voice came through the door.

"And John. I've brought my Bible. It seems you're in need of my services."

She turned wide eyes to Cal. "They wouldn't."

Cal swung his long, bare legs over the edge of the bed, grabbed the pair of denims she'd sneaked out of his room, and let out a ragged sigh. "It appears they have."

Chapter Fourteen

Cal hobbled to the door, spikes of pain jabbing his chest. He felt Jack's warmth as she came up behind him, murmuring under her breath. Slowly, he turned the knob.

Matt leaned against the doorjamb, something close to a smirk on his face. Behind him stood the others. Cal looked from face to face. Each stared back at him with fierce determination.

He pulled a hand over his face, stepping back to allow them in. No use doing this in the hallway. Despite the fresh bruises marring his face, Charley beamed at him as she stepped through the doorway. He suddenly had the uneasy feeling he was about to be plowed over.

Inwardly he smiled as Jack tapped her foot in agitation.

She glared. "Explain yourselves."

Alex stepped forward. "We believe the bounds of propriety have been breached."

Cal leaned against the closed door, his knees a bit weak. Alex turned his way. Her eyes went wide as his battered state registered. To her credit, she soldiered on, not saying a word about his condition.

"Bounds of propriety?" Jack said softly. The tight control of her words alerted Cal to the enormity of her distress.

He straightened, suddenly sensing the lot of them were deadly serious.

"You sir," Alex said, pointing at him, "have taken advantage of Jack's innocence. In the eyes of all other men, she is ruined. She'll never find a husband now."

Jack's cheeks bloomed with color, a bright crimson that also covered her neck and ears.

Guilt hit him hard. Alex was right. Although Jack had been raised unconventionally, she was still a lady and should be treated as such. If it were Charlotte who'd spent the night alone with a man, that man would have been strung up the nearest tree by now.

His gaze shot to a fuming Jack as Lou stepped forward. "Your reputation is ruined," she said.

"Now look here," Cal interrupted, angry at Jack's sisters' insinuations. "Say what you will about me, but I will not tolerate any maligning of Jack's character."

Charley cleared her throat. "What *I* say about *you* is that you're half naked. This looks quite compromising indeed. And I trust you'll do the right thing."

Jack stammered. "His clothes . . . the alley . . ." She broke off, apparently realizing any explanation was useless.

Cal caught the odd look between Matt and Reverend Hewitt, and he didn't like it one bit, especially when Matt said, "I'm convinced."

John Hewitt nodded, his expression grim. "Would you like the wedding performed here or in the library? Or perhaps the ballroom—it's still decorated."

"Wedding?" Jack said softly.

He turned to find her wide eyed. There was a look deep within her blue gaze that he couldn't identify.

"I think the ballroom will be lovely," Charley added.

Cal stared in complete and utter shock.

"Now, Jack," Alex said, "argue all you like, but you will marry Cal this morning."

Cal found this statement particularly interesting since Jack wasn't arguing at all. She had a dazed, lost look in her eyes as she stared at him.

Alex continued on, full force. "For once in our lives we are going to do the proper thing." She swallowed, then winced as she added, "Think of what Father would say if he knew you were alone with Cal for the night."

Cal bristled at Alex's manipulation. He could see the weakening in Jack's eyes.

He couldn't let this happen. She had her whole life ahead of her. Her ranch, her dreams. Being married to him . . . well it didn't fit with her plans, though the thought of her with him forever sounded more than a bit pleasing.

Jack looked at him, her blue eyes wide and unsure.

He breathed in. "No. There will not be a wedding. Not today, not ever."

The look of devastation in Jack's eyes shredded his heart. He hadn't wanted to hurt her, but if this was the only way . . . He pressed on. "I don't want a wife. They're nothing but trouble. And Jack? She's more trouble than most."

He stepped back, folded his arms, and waited for Jack to agree. After all, a marriage wasn't what she wanted. She wanted her ranch, her freedom.

Her nostrils flared. Her chin tipped up. Her eyes blazed. Cal stiffened as she turned to John Hewitt and said, "The ballroom will be perfect. I'll be ready in ten minutes and I'd appreciate a quick ceremony. I have somewhere to be." She stormed past Cal, and out the door, not even looking at him.

Matt clapped him on his shoulder. "Congratulations, pal. Looks like we're having ourselves a wedding."

"You look, er, lovely," Lou said, a grim smile marring her angelic features.

"Wouldn't you rather wear white?" Alex asked, fussing about the room. "We can fashion a gown for you in no time, using my wedding dress."

"No. This is fine."

'Trouble,' was she? Cal would just see how much trouble she could really cause.

She caught her lower lip between her teeth before its trembling revealed her true mood. Truth be told, she wished she could find a quiet corner and sob until all was right in her small world.

Married, to Cal? Elation is what she should be feeling. After all, this is what she wanted.

No, she amended silently. She wanted a marriage based on love. Shared love. Never in her wildest imaginings did she picture Cal forced against his will to marry her.

Closing her eyes, she thought back to the look she had seen in his eyes the night of the ball. There had been love in those green depths—she'd wager all she had on it. Why then? Why did he not want to marry her?

Anger rose in place of her sorrow. How dare he say she was trouble? She'd show him trouble. Trouble like he'd never known.

"Perhaps a dress at the very least." Alex hovered over her, looking more than a bit unnerved.

She looked down at herself. Black shirt, black pants, black boots. "No, this will do just fine."

Perhaps she was being a bit irrational, forcing this marriage on him. But the way he'd said he didn't ever want a wife took tight hold of something inside her and had yet to let go.

"A veil, then?"

Jack turned to Alex. "No, I want him to be able to see me." To see, and remember, what he was about to lose forever.

She almost felt sorry for her sisters. The looks on their faces told her that this wasn't quite the wedding they'd envisioned.

Somehow she couldn't summon any remorse. They had gotten her into this situation in the first place.

Lou smoothed Jack's hair, her touch gentle. "I don't think Cal meant to sound so . . . harsh."

"He meant it." The look in his eye had told her so. The green had turned hard as granite when he'd looked at her. She wanted to stomp her foot in frustration. Not five minutes before her meddling family had barged in, she would have sworn on a stack of Bibles that Cal loved her. Oh, he'd never said the words, but it had been there, in his eyes.

Was she just deluding herself into believing Cal had feelings for her? Seeing what she wanted to see?

Alex settled a slightly shaky hand on her arm. "Cal *is* a good bluffer, Jack."

Jack pondered that for a moment. Why would he bluff? What was there to gain from it other than to get out of marrying her?

No, he hadn't been bluffing. "Well, I'm about to call it, aren't I?"

Lou winced. "I wish you wouldn't think of it that way."

"How else am I to think of it?" she asked, hands on hips.

"You love him." Alex jabbed her finger in the air. "Don't try to deny it to us. We know you too well. This marriage might just be the best thing for both of you."

Jack turned toward the door. "It's best to get this over with. That's what's best."

A quick look at the clock showed the minutes slipping away. The sooner she left for the Searcy farm the better. Now that Cal had slipped away from her, her desire to buy the ranch had come back to her, tenfold. She just hoped the land was still available after missing her deadline yesterday, caring for Cal.

She didn't dare tell her sisters she planned to have this sham of a marriage annulled as soon as possible.

She wouldn't let Cal on to that fact, either. Let him suffer for a while.

"We better go," she said to her sisters. "I don't want to be late for my own wedding."

Three steps into the hallway a hand clamped around her arm. She stifled a gasp as a mutinous Cal stepped out of a shadowed doorway.

"Might I have a word with you?" His gaze shot over her shoulder to Alex and Lou. "Alone."

Alex stammered. "I, er, I don't think that's a good idea."

Pulling her arm from Cal's grasp, Jack turned to her sisters. "Go on ahead. Tell Matt and John we'll be right along."

"Are you sure?" Lou laid her small hand on Jack's arm. She looked as though she feared for Jack's safety. Not that Jack blamed her. The scowl on Cal's face, combined with his bruises, could frighten the hardest of souls. Thankfully, he didn't scare her.

"I'm sure," she said.

As soon as Alex and Lou had disappeared down the hall, Cal said, "You can't be serious, Jack. You don't really mean to go through with this, do you?"

Cold seeped into her bones with his distanced tone. "I certainly do." She edged her way down the hall, toward the ballroom. "Please pardon me if it causes you any *trouble.*"

"Dammit, Jack. I didn't mean it that way."

"What did you mean?"

He dragged his hand down his face, winced at the pain it must have caused. "I meant—" He paused. "I meant—"

She gave him a count of twenty in her head before she broke in. "That's what I thought."

She turned on her heel as her heart broke. All she wanted to hear from him was the truth, no matter what it might be. But most of all, she longed to see the same look on his face as earlier. The look that told her, above all else, that he cared for her. That his feelings ran deeper than he'd ever been able to speak.

Truth be told, when Alex had first mentioned this marriage, Jack's heart had leapt with joy. To have Cal as her husband . . .

Her joy had gone back into hiding when she'd seen Cal's face, his eyes, and knew it wasn't what he'd wanted as well.

Behind her Cal muttered under his breath, his footsteps heavy as he followed her. Ahead of her, voices carried out from the ballroom. She paused at the door, drawing in a deep breath. It was in her power to turn around, walk away.

Away from her wedding.

Away from Cal.

Why she stayed went beyond wanting to punish Cal.

It went to that joyous place in her heart rejoicing with the news of her becoming Cal's wife—if only for a little while.

"Let's go in," she said. "They're waiting for us."

Cal forced himself to relax. It didn't matter that he felt as though someone had just ran him up a flagpole.

For the love of man, she was wearing black to her own wedding. He'd thought she just hadn't changed yet. As she stood rigidly before him, it was abundantly clear that she had chosen the color on purpose. Pain sluiced through his chest. No doubt she was mourning the day she ever met him.

He kept his hands clenched tight, afraid he'd drag them over his face repeatedly wondering how it had come to this—a wedding.

His wedding.

Alex and Matt stood to the side, looking solemn. Lou stood at Jack's shoulder. To prevent her from escaping, he was sure.

Jack stood facing him, her eyes blazing as she repeated after John her part of the vows. He closed his eyes in frustration. He'd never mean to hurt her. He thought she'd think the idea of marrying was simply crazy.

Crazy for too many reasons.

And right for only one: he loved her. Loved every bit of her from each stubborn hair on her head to her booted toes.

He hadn't fallen in love with her beauty, although she was truly the most stunning woman he'd ever laid eyes on. It had been her sharp tongue, her quick laugh, the mischievousness in her eye that had lured her to him. But it had been her generous spirit, her loyalty, and her compassion that had captured his heart. If only he'd told her, his bride might actually look happy to marry him.

John Hewitt turned to him, his white collar seeming to glow. "Repeat after me: I, Carroll Lawrence McQue, take Jacquelyn Marie Parker as my lawfully wedded wife."

He didn't miss the jump of Jack's eyebrows at his name. He'd wager she'd never heard his given name before. And didn't that exemplify everything wrong with this wedding? That a bride didn't know her bridegroom's proper name?

Cal sincerely repeated the words, meaning them. He hoped Jack could hear the honesty in his voice.

Bible in hand, John turned to Jack. "Jack," he said, "Please repeat after me: I, Jacquelyn Marie Parker, take you Carroll Lawrence McQue to be my lawfully wedded husband."

Jack cleared her throat. For a second her mask of anger slipped and Cal saw the hurt lurking in her eyes and hated himself for putting it there.

"I, Jacquelyn Marie Parker, take you, Carroll Lawrence McQue, to be my awfully, er, lawfully wedded husband."

He knew darned well her slip hadn't been a mistake, and it was nothing less than he deserved.

"Yes, well," John murmured.

He finished the ceremony with due speed. "You, ahem, may now kiss your bride."

Jack bristled, but Cal pulled her close, trapping her in his arms. If he couldn't find the words to say it to her, so be it. He could certainly show her how he felt.

One arm locked around the small of her back, capturing her so she couldn't run. She didn't fight him, but she stood rigidly as she waited.

Although they were hardly alone, he felt as though

they were. The world could have fallen away around him and he wouldn't have noticed.

With his free hand he reached up and slid his fingers down the side of her face. Jack flinched at the touch. Her hot gaze shot to his. In her eyes, he saw confusion, anger . . . and something he was certain she wished remained hidden: desire. She wanted his touch as much as he wanted to touch her.

He kept his eyes open to watch her as he slowly, gently pressed a kiss to her temple. Barely taking his lips from her skin, he feathered kisses along her cheek, continuing down until his lower lip brushed against her upper one.

At the contact, she jerked back. He caught her, holding her close to his chest. He let her feel the pounding of his heart. When she looked up at him, he let her see all the love he held for her.

Her mouth parted in protest, and he took full advantage. He caught her bottom lip gently between his teeth, and he felt her sag against him.

Anchoring him to her, he deepened the kiss. Slowly, so slowly, she kissed him back. Inwardly he smiled. This was the woman he loved. How easily she could have fought against him, and he'd have let her go. Even in her anger, something inside her trusted him. And as he kissed her, he reveled in the fact that she wasn't so mad as to push him away.

In fact, somewhere along the way, her hands had snaked up around his neck, where she held on tight.

She wanted him, wanted his kiss, wanted his love. And it was all hers for the taking. All he had to do was explain. Explain everything and tell her what he should have told her weeks ago.

He loved her. So damn much it hurt.

She had to see that, *feel* that.

He heard her moan softly as he pushed his hand into her hair, his fingers tangling in the silkiness.

Through what felt like a drunken haze, he heard someone cough loudly. The sound barely registered until it was repeated with many 'Ahems' in its wake.

The noise must have broken through Jack's concentration as well, for she pulled back, stumbling away from him. He saw the confusion in her eyes as she rocked on the heels of her boots. He held her gaze, wanting her to see him. Him, her husband, the man who loved her more than all else in this world.

Her big eyes blinked, but she didn't look away. Dark hair swayed over her shoulder as she studied him, her lips still moist.

A single tear hovered at the corner of her eye as the words 'I love you' lodged in his throat. He needed to speak them, needed even more for her to hear them. To know how he felt about her.

He opened his mouth. "Jack, I—"

Her hair fanned out as she spun around and hurried toward the door. Abruptly she stopped when she reached Charley's side. Cal moved forward, his steps sluggish, as Jack grasped Charley's arms, spoke passionate words he couldn't hear.

He saw Charley nod, but before he could reach Jack's side, she was gone.

Charley had gone pale.

"What was that about?"

"Nothing," she said, not looking at him.

He heard a door slam somewhere down the corridor. He needed to go after Jack, to force her to listen to him. She was his now, and he was not letting her go.

It was clear Charley was keeping something from him, but he let it be. As he stood there he could very well see that she was not the little girl who needed his protection any longer. She had become a lovely young woman who could make her own choices in life.

He would always be her protector, but seeing her through Jack's eyes had changed him. Now he understood Charlotte's quest for independence, understood her desire to live life as she chose it. And he wouldn't deny her that right. If she wanted to run the Double C on her own, then he wouldn't stand in her way. He'd make sure she had all the help she needed and let her make her own decisions.

And he'd be free to be with Jack on her ranch. If Jack would have him.

He let out a sharp breath. The ranch! What had she said the other night . . .

That I'd pay in full by the end of the month— tomorrow. I'll ride out early and collect the deed.

The end of the month had been yesterday. But she hadn't left his side while caring for him.

Her words to John Hewitt rang in his head. *I'd appreciate a quick ceremony. I have somewhere to be.*

That 'somewhere' had to be the spread she was buying. His gut twisted. Would she lose the ranch? It would kill him if she missed out on fulfilling her dream because she'd been caring for him.

He sighed deeply. She was probably already on a horse headed out to River Glen. He wasn't going to sit here waiting for her to come back. He'd ride out there and meet her, tell her he loved her, and pray that she'd let him back into her life.

He set his hands on Charley's shoulders. "We need to speak, but first I need to find Jack."

She nodded, worrying her lip. Just what had Jack said to her that caused such apprehension? "I'll be here. And Cal?"

"Yes?"

"When you get back," she worried her hands, "there's someone I want you to meet. A man who's very special to me."

Shock rooted him to the floor. "A man?"

She nodded.

Closing his eyes, he took a deep breath. He'd known it, he supposed, all along. Had seen it in her demeanor. He reminded himself that she was a full-grown woman. One who could make her own decisions, choose the men in her life. Thanks to Jack, he could see that now. "I'd be honored to meet him."

"We'll be waiting in the library for you when you return." She smiled brightly. "Now go find Jack."

He kissed her forehead and rushed out the door.

Chapter Fifteen

Minx nickered, bringing Jack out of her thoughts. Blue skies shone above, birds sang, insects buzzed.

Holding the reins loosely, she allowed Minx the lead. She was in no rush to get to the ranch. She needed time to think, to make sure she was making the right decision.

Just a little time to decide what she wanted and if she had the courage to accept the gift of marriage she'd been given, in light of Cal's feelings on the matter.

In no time at all, she realized the decision had already been made—in her heart.

She was going to fight for her husband. Fight with all the love she held within. If that failed . . . Well, she couldn't let that happen, could she?

Cal was everything she wanted. More than any piece of land, more than any horse, he was all she needed.

Sure, she'd been determined to hate him for making her so miserable. Determined to harden her heart against him. Until his kiss. A kiss like no other. One that singed her to the core of her being, turned her heart to ash.

And the look he'd given her afterward? The one full of promises, of hopes?

Her thoughts, her plans, had been scattered in a dozen different directions since, but only one notion stuck.

She loved him with every breath she took, and couldn't—wouldn't—live without him.

She just needed to convince him that he needed her as much.

Wild grass grew high on the side of the shade-dappled road. Large maples rose like giant guards on her left side, while to her right, land stretched out endlessly, full of possibilities.

She urged Minx forward. Jack's thick braid thumped her back as Minx covered the uneven road without a hitch. As they crested a hill, the Searcy farm came into view. Jack looked at it through disillusioned eyes, feeling oddly detached.

Weeks ago, excitement had filled her blood, drowned her with anticipation of owning her own spread. But now . . .

She gnawed on her lower lip as Minx's lazy steps brought her closer to a dream that no longer held the promise of her future.

No, that promise had been altered the moment she'd said, 'I do.' And meant it.

All too quickly, she could call to memory the kisses he'd given her. The tender words, the soft caresses, and the unspoken promises.

Alex's words rang in her head. *Cal is a good bluffer, Jack.*

Jack's heart—and her future—depended on it being true.

She guided Minx with a click of her tongue and a tap of her heel down the gravel lane leading to the Searcy farmhouse.

Jack pulled back on the reins in front of the weathered porch. "Mr. Searcy?" she called out, announcing her arrival as she dismounted. "It's Jack Parker."

The door to the farmhouse squeaked open. Mr. Searcy came out, wiping his hands on his pants. "Miss Parker," he said, solemnly.

She smiled. "Don't look so glum, Mr. Searcy."

He wobbled down the front steps. "But Miss Parker, the land . . . When you never showed yesterday . . . Well, I sold it this morning."

Minx pawed the dirt with her hoof. Jack ran her hand down the horse's neck. "I figured you would. We did have a deal—one I didn't uphold."

His eyes widened. "You aren't angry? I thought you had yer head set on this land."

She looked across the small valley, at the acres and acres before her. "I did. But," she said softly, "my heart had other designs." She scuffed her boot on the ground, sending plumes of dust upward. "I came to tell you in person that I needed to rescind my offer—in case you hadn't sold the land and had been waiting for me."

He nodded, his chins jiggling. "I see. I'll set about gathering up your money then."

"Our original deal holds true, Mr. Searcy. You may take a portion of my offer for your trouble."

He winked. "No trouble a'tall. In truth, once peoples learnt I'd already accepted a bid, their bids rose higher n' higher. I got myself one fine deal. You did me a favor, you did."

"I'm glad. Really, I am."

He turned on shaky legs, went up the steps. "I'll be just a minute."

Jack saw to Minx, making sure she was watered. Mr. Searcy came out, handed her an envelope containing her down payment.

"Thank you," she said, tucking it into the saddlebag.

"I be hopin' these designs your heart have make you right happy."

She shook his heavy hand. "I hope so too. Do you mind," she said to him, "if I take a moment?" She motioned toward the fields.

"Be my guest, Miss Parker. It's been a pleasure."

Jack said her good-byes, tethered Minx, and wandered down a steep embankment to the corral below. Weeds choked the ground, growing up and out, twisting around the wooden posts of the fence, covering her boots.

She braced her weight as she imagined horses inside the corral—her horses.

It would have been nice. And she silently admitted she wasn't ready to give up the notion of having her own ranch one day, but she knew for certain this particular ranch hadn't been for her. Not at the cost of losing Cal.

The thick grass grabbed at her boot heels as she circled the fence.

Dandelions swayed at her feet. She bent down, plucked one from the dry earth.

Closing her eyes, she thought about a wish. Thought not with her head, but with her heart.

It was an easy wish to make.

Inhaling, she drew in a deep breath, let it out slowly through tight lips. Dandelion fluff danced in the sunlight as it was blown from the stem. Jack watched as the wind caught the small flecks and carried them gently to the ground. Her gaze stretched out across the meadows, the rolling hills.

"Jack!"

Her head snapped at the sound of her name.

Up the hill, Cal stood, dressed in black from head to toe, hands on hips. She tugged down the brim of her hat as the sun beat down behind him, making him look more than a bit like an avenging angel.

Her heart leapt at the same time her stomach clenched. She started toward him as he came down the hill. As she neared, she saw the unmistakable look of determination in his green eyes.

She swallowed. "What are you doing here? You shouldn't have been riding—you're healing." His pain, she reflected, must have been intense.

"You weren't too late, were you?" he asked, a hint of desperation in his voice.

"Late?"

His warm hand settled on the small of her back as he guided her up the incline. "Your deadline was yesterday."

Disappointment coursed through her. He was here about the ranch. Just about the ranch. She should have known his sense of decency would have him feeling guilty.

"Mr. Searcy sold the ranch to someone else."

His head dropped. "I'm so sorry, Jack. It's all my fault. Perhaps if I had a word with him . . ."

He started toward the front porch, but she held him back. "Your fault? How?"

"If you hadn't been taking care of me, you wouldn't have missed your deadline."

She folded her arms across her chest. "I wasn't anywhere I didn't want to be. Besides, it no longer matters."

"How can you say that? This ranch was all you ever wanted."

"Not so," she said, edging away from him. She ran her hand over Minx's sleek belly.

He grabbed her arm. "What do you mean by that?"

Was that hope she heard in his voice? She searched his gaze, finding nothing in the green depths to confirm her thoughts.

She needed to lay her heart out and hope he didn't trample it. Honesty was the only way out of her current misery. She owed that much to him.

She rubbed down the horse he'd ridden, a chocolate bay with expressive eyes.

"Jack." He stilled her hand, capturing it with his own. "What did you mean by the ranch not being all you ever wanted?"

The strings to her hat swayed against her chest as she looked up at him. "Why did you come here?"

"You know why." His fingers sent pulses of heat shooting into her veins.

"The ranch. Is that all?"

Releasing her arm, he sighed. His eyes softened. "You know it's not. We need to talk about this morning."

A part of her feared what he had to say. Yet another part danced with hope.

Jack checked on Minx, adjusted her saddle and bags. Cal stepped up behind her, the heat of his chest burrowing into her spine, where it tunneled through the rest of her, all the way to her toes.

"I'm sorry I hurt you," he said.

She fiddled with the buckles on the saddles, not wanting to face him.

His breath caressed her neck. "I never meant to do that."

Sudden desire had her wanting to back into him, to feel his body pressed against hers, head to toe. She yearned to feel his touch, here, there, everywhere. She wanted to be his. And she wanted him to be hers.

Her heart in her throat, she said, "What do you want?"

He ran his fingers down the backs of her arms, raising hope along with gooseflesh in their wake. She shivered.

"I wasn't sure at first. And then seeing Charley standing in the back of the ballroom reinforced my decision. You were right about her, as you've been right about many things. She's become a woman without me noticing." He chuckled. "She even has someone she wants me to meet. A beau, I daresay."

Jack spun. She gripped his shirt. "What?"

Confusion dipped his eyebrows. "Charley has someone she wants me to meet. Said she'd be waiting for me in the library when we got back to the boat."

"Oh, Lord." Jack fought against the sudden onslaught of emotions threatening her determination. The anger at Charley for not doing as she'd asked in keeping away from Daley Lombard until she returned, the guilt about not having told Cal about the man's presence in the first place.

His hands gripped her shoulders. "What is it?"

Her eyelids fluttered closed. She should have told him the moment she realized . . . She broke free of his hands, jumped into the saddle. "It's Daley Lombard, Cal."

His eyes widened. "What about him?"

"He's here. In town. *He's* Charley's beau."

With stormy eyes, Cal jumped on his horse, kicking the bay into motion. "Like hell he is."

As Jack followed Cal's breakneck pace, she could only hope Charley hadn't done anything foolish.

Chapter Sixteen

Cal's heart hammered in his ears as he stormed up the *Amazing Grace's* stage.

Jack's boot heels clicked behind him, matching him step for step as he yanked open the doors leading into the lobby of the boat, and took the stairs two at a time.

He flinched when he felt her hand settle on his arm, dragging him to a stop.

"You can't go in there like this," she said, her voice gentle, yet firm.

"Why not?" he bellowed. Her eyebrows shot up. He cleared his throat, tried again in a respectable tone. "Why not?"

"She's in love with him, Cal."

They'd been through this on the ride home. Jack had explained all she knew, yet he still couldn't grasp the fact that his sister had fallen for the phony charms of Daley Lombard.

"She's mistaken," he said, grinding his heel into the carpet.

"I don't think so."

He stared at her. She lifted her chin, stared back.

Lord in heaven, how he wanted to take her in his arms, hold her forever.

Soon, he promised himself. Soon enough he'd tell her how much he loved her and make things right between them.

But right now he had to deal with Charley.

And Daley Lombard. He was lucky that Cal's gun had been stolen.

"Her heart is going to be broken when she learns of that promissory note. She needs your support right now, your compassion. Not your anger."

He paced the thickly carpeted hallway. "It's not her with whom I'm angry."

"No, it's the man she loves. Which, quite possibly, could be worse." She shrugged. "I can't tell you how badly I wanted to hunt down those men who hurt you and hang them by their toenails."

He smiled, said softly, "Does that mean you love me, Jack?" His chest tightened with the sudden need to know if it was true or not. He'd work his way through this mess with Charley. But he didn't know what he would do without Jack in his life.

She blinked at him, her cheeks coloring. "We can discuss that later, when we have more time."

What did that mean? he wondered. Her usually expressive eyes gave nothing away as she continued on, apparently oblivious to his heartache. "You need to walk into that library as calm and level-headed as you please. Present your case with a rational, detached tone."

"Said just like the daughter of a judge."

"I learned from the best. You need to trust me." She looked up at him, all blue eyes in her small, heart-shaped face. "Do you?"

"Do I?"

"Trust me?"

"With everything." Including his heart. But he didn't dare say so—yet. It struck him then that for the first time in weeks, his head didn't hurt. Tension, the doctor had said. At this moment, tension filled him from top to bottom, but there was a difference now.

Jack was by his side. Forever, if he had any say about it.

One of her dark eyebrows arched. "You'll be calm?"

He couldn't help the joy he felt. With her here by his side, he could do anything. "I'll try."

She held out her hand, palm up. "I'll help."

He slipped his hand over hers, held tight. Something deep inside twisted. How could he have ever thought he could live without her?

She smiled, nearly knocking the all the air from his chest. "Let's go."

The library doors stood open at the far end of the hall.

Jack squeezed his hand. He fought against pulsating anger, wondering how long he could hold it in.

If Lombard had done anything to Charley . . .

His breath caught as he walked in and saw the two of them, their heads bent close together as they sat on a long sofa.

When Charley saw him, she jumped up. Cal locked eyes with Lombard, daring the man to make one false move. A move that would allow Cal to unleash his anger.

A tremulous smile played on Charley's lips. Her gaze jumped to his hand, entwined with Jack's. However the normal cheer in her voice had been greatly tempered as she said, "How wonderful! You found Jack! I assume everything is well?"

Cal grit his teeth. "Don't make assumptions, Charlotte."

She sighed. "I do so like it better when you call me Charley."

Jack's thumb slid over his knuckles. He turned to look at her. A wealth of compassion weighed in the depths of her deep blue eyes.

"I—I," Charley stammered. "I don't suppose I need to make introductions."

"I suppose not," Jack murmured. She nodded. "Mr. Lombard."

Cal bit back a growl as Lombard set a hand on the small of Charley's back and said, "Cal, Mrs. McQue, my felicitous respects on your wedding. Congratulations."

"Thank you," Jack said. She elbowed Cal in the midsection.

"Thank you," he bit out.

"Let's sit." Charlotte smoothed imaginary wrinkles from her pants. She smiled brightly, too brightly. "Tell us about your reconciliation."

Jack tugged on his hand, led him to the sofa across from his sister and that . . . that scoundrel. She practically forced him to sit, but she never released his hand. She was his anchor, grounding him during this current storminess.

"This isn't the time, Charlotte," he said, "as you well know. It's time to stop stalling."

"First things first," Daley Lombard said, reaching behind the sofa.

"I don't believe I want to hear anything you have to say, Lombard."

Charley's pale eyebrows snapped together. "Cal!

There's no need to be rude. Not at all. One might question your manners."

"Yes," Jack murmured. "One might."

He stole a glance at her, found her smiling.

Cal gave himself a good mental shake. Having Jack here was both good and bad. She calmed him, held him in line. Without her here, Lombard might be a corpse on the floor by now. Yet having her here clouded his senses. His attention tended to wander to her, just to look at her, drink his fill of her smooth skin and bottomless eyes.

His gaze dropped to the table between them, piled high with books. Alongside the various tomes, Lombard had placed a moneybag. In his hand, he held a gun.

He leaned forward, set it on the stack of books. "I don't blame you if you want to shoot me with it, but I do hope you'll listen to what I have to say before you do."

Jack gasped and turned to Cal with a question in her eyes. "Isn't that your gun?"

Lombard nodded to the moneybag. "That's yours too. All of it. Plus some extra for a belated wedding gift, courtesy of O'Malley's patrons."

Suspicion leapt forward. "How'd you get this?" Cal asked, taking the six-shooter from the table and turning it over in his palm. No doubt, it was his.

"Charley told me what happened to you. I felt it only right that your money be returned to you."

"But how? Those men wouldn't just hand it over."

"I'm also the son of a gambling man, Cal. Or have you forgotten?"

Hah! Forgotten? Not likely. It was the reason they were all here, wasn't it?

"I'm so sorry, Cal," Charley said, tears welling in her eyes.

Cal felt Jack's arm snake around his back, her fingers dancing along his spine in silent support. His jaw ticked. "Why are you sorry, Charlotte?"

"It's my fault."

"What is?"

"That you were beaten."

"No," Lombard interrupted. "The blame is entirely my own. If I hadn't gone to Cal with that blasted note . . ."

Cal surged forward, but Jack's strong hand kept him from gaining his feet. His gaze darted to his sister. "You knew about the note?"

"I've always known about it. Ever since Father wrote it. But I never wanted you to know about it. Unfortunately, I knew how you would react."

His stomach knotted. "I don't understand. Any of this. Lombard came to me with the note, demanded payment due. Are you telling me you knew of that?"

Sunlight pored into the room, sending fingers of light racing across the carpeting. A tear slid down Charley's cheek. "No. I didn't know that. Not until yesterday. Daley came to you without my knowledge. Nor did I know about your quest to raise that money. If I had, I'd have done something to stop it. All of this was quite preventable."

"See," Lombard said, leaning forward, "I thought I was making the right decision." He clasped his hands together. "It didn't dawn on me that you would try to earn that much money in that short amount of time. The note was simply supposed to get you to agree to let me marry Charlotte. We were going to come to you this week, ask your blessing."

Cal bit his lip to keep from saying 'over my dead

body'. He'd told Jack he'd hear them through. As painful as it was turning out to be.

"He doesn't know you as I do, Cal," Charley said. "Now I understand why you insisted I come with you here. Why you've spent your days and nights in gaming halls. I thought you were simply escaping into the cards—I didn't know the extent of your gambling. I had no reason to suspect since I didn't know the foolish lengths Daley had gone to." She swallowed. "I'm so sorry."

Lombard flushed a deep red. "I might have put two and two together," he said, "but Charlotte made no mention of your gaming forays until the night you disappeared."

Cal shook his head. "I still don't understand. Why? Why was all this necessary?"

"We're in love, Cal," Charley said, her voice sure, her eyes clear. "We've been in love for years."

"No."

"Yes. You haven't been there. You haven't seen it."

"He's just using you," Cal countered. "He wants the land."

Long blond locks fell forward as she shook her head. "No."

Jack's thumb made lazy sweeps between his shoulder blades. He set his hand on her thigh, needing to touch her, needing her strength to help him through this.

"How can you say that, Charley? All our lives the Lombards have wanted your land. Why has that suddenly changed? You're wearing blinders, Charlotte, and it's time to take them off."

Jack's hand stilled for just a moment and he drew in a deep breath, trying to rein in the anger, the accusations. It took every ounce of restraint he had to sit still and watch Daley Lombard lift his sister's hand, tuck it into his own.

And the look he gave her?

Hell.

Lombard looked at Charley the way he himself looked at Jack. The way Matt looked at Alex. The way his father had looked at his mother.

It wasn't possible. Was it?

Lombard's voice held more than a hint of anger as he said, "Our fathers cast long shadows, McQue. Shadows we both withered under for many years. It took me a long while to find my own path, as I presume," he nodded to Jack, "that you've found yours."

Charley leaned forward. "Daley's sold all the Lombard holdings, including the property bordering ours. We want to live on the Double C. We want to sell the cattle and farm a little, but mostly we want to build a workshop where Daley can hone his craft." Her eyes teared. "He makes the most wonderful furniture."

Cal's eyes widened in shock. If he'd sold the land, then there was no motive to marrying Charley . . . except for love.

"It's true," Charley pressed on. "He wants to separate himself from his father, who his father had been, what he had done."

"I made a mistake coming to you with that note, and I'm man enough to admit so." Lombard didn't so much as blink when he spoke. "It was an ill-conceived plan, but I didn't want to risk losing Charlotte. Beyond knowing you wouldn't approve of a marriage between us, there was your request that Charlotte be twenty-five before she weds hanging over our heads. An eternity from now. So I stooped to my father's level to guarantee the result I wanted, never thinking of the consequences you might face in trying to raise the money."

Stooping was a feeling Cal knew all too well. Still . . . "I don't know what to think."

Charley's green eyes pleaded. "I hope that you're thinking that for once in your life you could be wrong. That you've judged a man unfairly. That mistakes can be made."

"And forgiven," Jack said, rising to her feet.

He locked gazes with her, realizing there was still much left unsaid between them. To Charley, he said, "I need time to think this through."

Their hands still linked, Charley and Daley rose. "Fair enough," she said. "Tomorrow?"

"Charley," he warned as she hurried toward the door.

Lombard stopped as Charley turned the handle. He looked back, his dark eyes solemn. "How long are we to carry the sins of our fathers?" With that, he followed Charley from the room.

Cal's gaze dropped to the table. He picked up his gun. He smiled. "I still want to shoot him."

Jack laughed. "Charley would never forgive you."

He tucked the gun into his boot. "I suppose you're right."

Jack crossed the room to look out the window. Cal came up behind her, putting his hands on her shoulders. The river glistened in the sunlight.

"They're in love. You can see it in the way they look at each other," she said.

"I don't have to like it, do I?"

She turned, looked up at him. "No, you don't. But I do think you have to accept it."

She was right, and he knew it. If he didn't give his blessing, Charlotte would marry Daley despite his wishes. He'd seen it in her eyes, in the set of her chin. He'd allow Daley Lombard into the family. For Charley, he would. But it would be a long time before he welcomed him. Sometimes the older the wound the harder to heal. "I'll give them my blessing tomorrow."

Long dark lashes hid her eyes. He nudged up her chin. "What about us?" he asked, laying his heart bare.

She blinked, then wet her lips. "Us?"

"We still need to talk."

He felt her shudder as she drew in a deep breath. "Yes, we do."

"Now is as good a time as any."

She shook her head, sending her braid flying. "No. I need time."

His heart sank. "How much?"

"Meet me tonight."

"When?"

"Midnight in the gaming hall."

On second thought, having time benefited him. There were a few things he needed to see to. "I'll be there."

"Oh, and Cal?"

"Hmm?"

She smiled. "Bring a deck of cards."

Chapter Seventeen

As Jack walked into the room, Cal stood. She closed the door behind her. His bruised eye had turned from a dark bluish to a deep purple dotted with yellows. His green gaze locked onto her, watching her every breath.

Her chest tightened. It would all be over soon. "Are you ready?" she asked. He tugged out a chair, guiding her into it. The warmth of his hand seeped through her shirt. Tiny sparks of awareness danced across her skin, and she knew she was doing the right thing. He settled in across from her.

His rough voice washed over her senses. "Yes."

"I've brought paper," she said.

"Why?"

"Our wagers."

His dark eyebrows arched in question.

She took the deck of cards from him and shuffled while she explained. "Write down what you want. Whether to end our marriage or what have you. Write it down, put it in the kitty."

Arched eyebrows dove into a scowl. His hand came

across the table to settle on hers. "Are you sure about this?"

Knots twisted in her stomach. She was never surer about anything in her whole life. She looked at him, straight on. "Absolutely."

He tugged a piece of paper loose from the pad, lifted the pencil, and looked at her for a long, long moment.

This wasn't a time for bluffing. It took all her courage not to turn away from his pointed gaze, not show her feelings.

She was scared to death.

Scared she was going to lose him forever. A notion that didn't sit well with her. Not at all.

The rough scratching of the pencils against paper seemed to echo across the room. One lamp cast a soft glow as Jack wrote down what she wanted. Carefully, she folded the paper, set it in the center of the table.

A muscle ticked in Cal's jaw. "What are we playing?"

Cards slipped through Jack's fingers. "We're cutting. Aces high." She swallowed. "Hearts are wild."

He nodded as she set the deck on the table. He cut the deck in half and Jack fanned the cards out across the tabletop.

"You first," she said.

She watched as his long, strong fingers danced along the cards. Finally, he pulled one free, dragged it over to him. He lifted the corner of the card, and Jack's gaze shot to his eyes, where a small spark jumped to life.

Her heart sank. He obviously had a good card. Her gaze fell to the table, where his folded piece of paper lay. She wished with all her might she could see what he had written, to know for certain he wanted the same thing she did. But she didn't.

Not knowing spurred her into doing something so terrible, so wrong, that she couldn't stop to think about it or she'd never be able to go through with it.

She reached out, ran her fingers over the cards, pulled one loose.

Sliding it toward her, she swallowed hard, unable to believe what she'd just done. She lifted the corner though she knew what card she held.

Wetting her lips, she looked at Cal. Her throat tightened around words she knew she ought to be saying, choking them off. Words of love.

She nodded to him. Slowly he turned his card over, a triumphant smile on his face. A king of spades.

Biting her lip, she slowly turned over her own card, fighting hard to keep her hand from trembling.

The ace of hearts.

She heard Cal's sharp intake of breath, felt his disappointment. Tears sprang to her eyes.

"Well then," he said. "Let's see what we've got here."

As he reached for the folded notes, Jack's hand covered his. "I'm sorry if you're disappointed."

He tipped his head to the side, studied her. "We'll have to see about that, won't we?"

Jack squared her shoulders, lifted her chin as Cal unfolded the paper on which she had written two short words. She held tight onto the tears brimming in her eyes.

Cal unfolded the last corner, read the words. His gaze jumped to her, then back to the paper as if he couldn't believe what he'd just read. His voice strained, he said, "Are you serious?"

"I've never been more so."

He leaned back in his chair, let his head fall back. Her nerves jumped with every deep breath he took. When he straightened, he looked at her, moisture clinging to his long dark lashes.

An intolerable ache built in her chest. She couldn't do this to him. She couldn't make him do something he didn't want. Especially since she hadn't played their little game fairly.

"Cal, I—"

His laughter interrupted her. Setting his elbows on the table, he put his head in his hands and laughed.

Watching him, she sat back in her chair, wondering what in the world he found so funny.

Slowly, he looked up at her, brushed tears from his face. "You thought I'd be disappointed?"

"I didn't know," she said softly. "I still don't."

He edged his wager to her side of the table. "Read it."

She didn't want to know. Really, she didn't. "It's not necessary."

"I think it is."

The tone of his voice, the soft, gentle prodding spurred her to lift the paper, unfold its edges. She closed her eyes, took a deep breath before opening them again. There was but one word written on the paper.

You.

Tears built as she read it over and over again. Before she knew he'd even risen from his chair, Cal knelt down next to her.

She looked at him through blurry eyes.

He cupped her cheek. "You. All I've ever wanted was you."

She fell off her chair and into his arms. For a long while, she let him hold her, rock her. When she finally felt as though her voice would work, she pulled back, but remained in his arms.

With gentle caresses, she stroked his face, around his bruised eye, down his jaw line. Unable to stand it a moment more, she slowly lowered her head, sought his lips with hers.

Though she meant the kiss to be soft and full of promises and love, it quickly turned heated. Fireworks, it seemed, exploded inside her. Behind her closed eyes, bright colors swam, and small explosions rocked the very center of her being.

She wanted more. She wanted everything.

Pulling back, she gasped for air, fought for control. His chest heaved and she put her hands on it, feeling his wild heartbeat. She reveled in the knowledge that he was equally as affected as she.

She looked deep into his darkened eyes, spoke the words her soul had yearned to say for so long. "I love you. So very much I love you."

He brought her toward him for another kiss, this one soft and searching yet just as shattering to her senses.

"I've tried to tell you so many times just how much I love you, but I could never voice the words. They hung there," he said, "in my heart day after day. And I'm sorry."

Her heart hammered. "Why?"

"Because if I'd said them sooner, we could have had this happiness sooner." He took a deep breath. "I love you, Jack. Oh, how I love you."

She placed her fingers against his lips. "We have now. And we have tomorrow. And we have forever."

A smile curved under her fingertips. "So you want a baby, do you?"

A baby.

It was what she had written for her wager. There

was nothing she wanted more than to have a baby with this man. This man who loved her.

A broad smile tugged at her cheeks. "Actually, I want many, many children, but I didn't want to press my luck."

He laughed, rose to his feet and tugged her up with him. "I think we can manage that. Not only that, but a big ranch to raise them on as well."

"What? How?"

Cal pulled a piece of paper from his pocket. "I've been thinking . . ."

"About?"

He captured her gaze with his dark green eyes. "You've always dreamed of ranching—"

She broke in. "But I know you don't care for—"

He cut her off. "What is it *I've* always dreamed of doing?"

She sighed. She sensed he was going somewhere with this, but hadn't any idea where. "Owning your own saloon or gaming hall. But we both know you can't do that around here—not with your name."

"Exactly."

"Cal, I love you, really I do, but you're confusing the devil out of me."

He unfolded the paper. "I saw this the other day in that magazine of yours while you were sleeping."

She frowned at the advertisement of Montana land Cal had cut out. "What's this?"

"Our future."

Hope flared in her chest, billowed out. "How?"

"There's this town—Willow Creek; a small town near to brand new. There's a jail, a small general store, a railroad office and a hotel. And a saloon whose owner is looking to move farther west. He's put his establishment up for sale. And right on the outskirts of town—he tapped the advertisement—there's land for sale. Land enough to build a fine ranch house, raise some horses . . . and some babies."

She could barely believe what she was hearing. All she ever wanted, including the man she loved, was within her grasp.

"What do you think?" he asked.

"I think I love you. And I think it's a wonderful idea. Let's do it."

He wrapped his arms around her, tugging her close. While safe in his arms, she thought about her sisters and how much she would miss them. Both Lou and Alex knew how Jack longed to move West—and she knew they wouldn't begrudge her decision to leave. Yet that wouldn't stop Jack from missing them terribly.

She gnawed her lower lip, pulled back slightly to look up at him. "You did say there was a railroad?"

He nodded. "Stops right in town."

Trips to and from Cincinnati would be of little difficulty.

"Jack?"

Feeling just the slightest bit overwhelmed, she moved back into her husband's arms. "I'm going to miss them, is all."

His soothing hands caressed her spine. "We can find somewhere closer . . ."

"Nearly all my life I've dreamed of living in Montana. I gave it up because I didn't think I could go it alone. But with you by my side, I can do anything. Go anywhere. Fulfill all my dreams. I'll tell my sisters tomorrow."

He held her close. His heart beat steadily against her chest. The boat rocked slightly, and the tall grandfather clock in the corner of the gaming hall chimed once.

"It's getting late," she said, suddenly unsure about what to do next. It was, after all, her wedding night.

"I have something for you."

"You do?"

Cal stooped under the table, pulled out a fancily wrapped box. "Open it," he said.

She bit her lip as she tugged on colored ribbon. She set the paper aside, lifted the box top. Underneath a layer of fine tissue, lay the most beautiful garment Jack had ever seen.

She pulled the white silk nightgown from the box and held it in front of her. Thin straps dangled from her fingers as the silk slid over her hands, draped her body.

She looked to her husband, a smile on her lips. "You were rather confident you'd be winning tonight."

He grinned. "I play to win, Jack. You wore black to our wedding, but you'll be wearing white on our wedding night."

Heat bloomed in her face at his bold talk. Yet she loved every word. Carefully, she placed the nightgown back into the box and tucked the package it under one arm.

Cal held out his hand. "Let's go to bed."

She smiled, slipping her hand into his. "Let's."

As they walked toward the door, Cal paused and said, "If I were a gambling man, I'd suspect a little tampering with those cards tonight. An ace of hearts? The likeliness of you drawing that is next to nothing."

Jack bit back her growing smile, tugging on the door handle. She turned to look at him, all the love she felt glowing in her eyes. "A wise man once told me that some things, Cal, are worth cheating for."

Epilogue

A fire blazed in the marble hearth, sending waves of warmth out into the large room, furnished with only two small couches and four armchairs. The rest of the room was as bare as the day John Hewitt had bought it.

Dark clouds promising snow hung outside the windows as Jack considered her family.

Alex and Matt sat together on one sofa, Lou and John on the other. Cal sat in the chair next to hers, his hand resting on her thigh. Charley and Daley sat side by side on the hearth, holding hands. They had traveled up from Louisville and were staying on the *Amazing Grace* for the holiday weekend.

The scent of roasted turkey filled the room, making Jack's stomach rumble. She hoped to heaven above that Cora, John and Lou's housekeeper, had made the Thanksgiving dinner, not Lou herself. The memory of Lou nearly poisoning an unsuspecting John would linger for a long while, she supposed.

Alex chattered on about how successful the *Amazing Grace* had been during the summer months, how the monthly themed balls were also a huge triumph.

182

"How is the house coming?" Jack asked her sister.

Matt groaned. Alex elbowed him. "It's coming along nicely."

Alex and Matt had bought a small house on the outskirts of the city. Close enough to the river for daily trips to the *Amazing Grace,* but also in a lovely area for their little girl to grow and play in.

Jack took in an eyeful of her small niece, just weeks old. Cuddled in Jack's arms, Autumn Rose Kinkade blinked up at her with her mother's big brown eyes. Her little chin, complete with her father's cleft, shot into the air and Jack smiled. She might have the name Kinkade, but this little one was a Parker through and through.

Jack and Cal had dropped everything to board the first train out of Willow Creek when they received word of Autumn Rose's birth.

Jack had left the running of her thriving ranch in the capable hands of Grogan, and Cal had set the sign on his saloon to "Closed—due to Autumn Rose Kinkade."

Willow Creek's only doctor, an aging Indian medicine man, assured Jack it was safe to travel in the early months of her pregnancy, that her baby would be safe.

Their baby. Hers and Cal's.

For nearly a month now, she'd dreamed nightly of the little boy she carried. She could see him clear as day, with Cal's green eyes and her dark hair. She laughed inwardly, sure she was bound to have a girl to carry on the tradition, despite the dreams. She'd be more than pleased with either.

Autumn Rose squirmed in Jack's arms, and she passed the small baby off to Cal.

Without a trace of nervousness, he set the baby in the crook of his arm and cooed to her.

Jack took a deep breath, willing those darned tears to remain at bay. Watching him hold the baby made her love him all the more—if it were possible.

"See here, Reverend," Daley said. "I know where you could find a great bargain on furniture."

Dog, John and Lou's dog, growled low in his throat. With a pat, John pacified the cranky mutt. He smiled. "Think I need some, do you?"

Lou's face lit. "A few additional pieces might be nice. And I hear your work is beautiful."

As they chatted on, Jack took in Lou's healthy glow. In addition to singing as Madame Angelique on the *Amazing Grace,* she'd taken on quite a few of John's charities and loved every minute she spent helping others.

Jack tipped her head to the side repeatedly, trying to get Lou's attention with no success.

"Lou, I do believe Jack is going to give herself a broken neck if you don't look at her," Charley said, laughing.

"Oh!" Lou jumped to her feet at Jack's motioning.

Alex leaned forward. "What are the two of you up to?"

"We have a present for Autumn Rose, Jack and I." Lou drew an envelope from her pocket. The hem of her skirt swirled about her ankles as she crossed the room and set the paper in Alex's hand.

Alex looked up, her brown eyes puzzled.

Jack sat on the edge of Cal's chair. His warm hand settled on her back, soothing her, as she said, "It's our gift to Autumn Rose for her baptism."

"But you gave her gifts already," Alex protested.

Lou sighed. "Just open it."

Matt leaned over Alex's shoulder as she pulled back the flap on the envelope and drew out the slip of paper inside.

Alex gasped. Her hand flew to her mouth. "But you can't!"

"We can," Lou said.

Jack added, "And we want to. It's rightfully hers."

Alex shook her head, her curls bouncing. "No, we can't accept it."

Jack had known Alex wouldn't accept this particular gift easily. "It's too late. Lou and I have already had it notarized. Our two-thirds ownership of the *Amazing Grace* now belongs to Autumn Rose."

Lou knelt down next to Alex. "Almost a year ago, Matt bought the boat rightfully. He should have never let Jack and I retain partial ownership as he did."

Alex sniffled. "It was our gift to both of you."

Jack stood, went to her sisters. "Now it's our gift to our niece."

Jack thought back to the day of her father's funeral, to the day she learned about the *Amazing Grace*. She wondered if her father had known the joy his gift to them would bring into their lives.

Thanks to the steamboat their father left behind, all three of them had found self-fulfillment, independence, adventure . . . and enough love to last a lifetime.

Tears welled and she didn't hold them back or care who saw them because what had happened to the three of them . . . Well, Jack reflected, it was nothing short of amazing.